I0729296

A VALLEY CHRISTMAS

A MORGAN'S RUN ROMANCE

M. LEE PRESCOTT

A Valley Christmas

By
M. Lee Prescott

Published by Mt. Hope Press
Copyright 2019, M. Lee Prescott
Cover Design by Ashley Lopez
Formatting by E-book Formatting Fairies
ISBN: 978-1-7330217-1-5

All rights reserved. No part of this publication may be reproduced, stored, or transmitted (auditory, graphic, mechanical, or electronic) without the express written permission of the author, except in the case of brief quotations or excerpts used in critical reviews or articles. Thank you for respecting the hard work of this author. To obtain permission to excerpt portions of the text, please contact the author at *mleeprescott@gmail.com*

http://www.mleeprescott.com/

This book is a work of fiction. Names, characters, places, and events are products of the author's imagination or are used fictitiously. Any resemblance to actual people (alive or deceased), locales, or events is entirely coincidental.

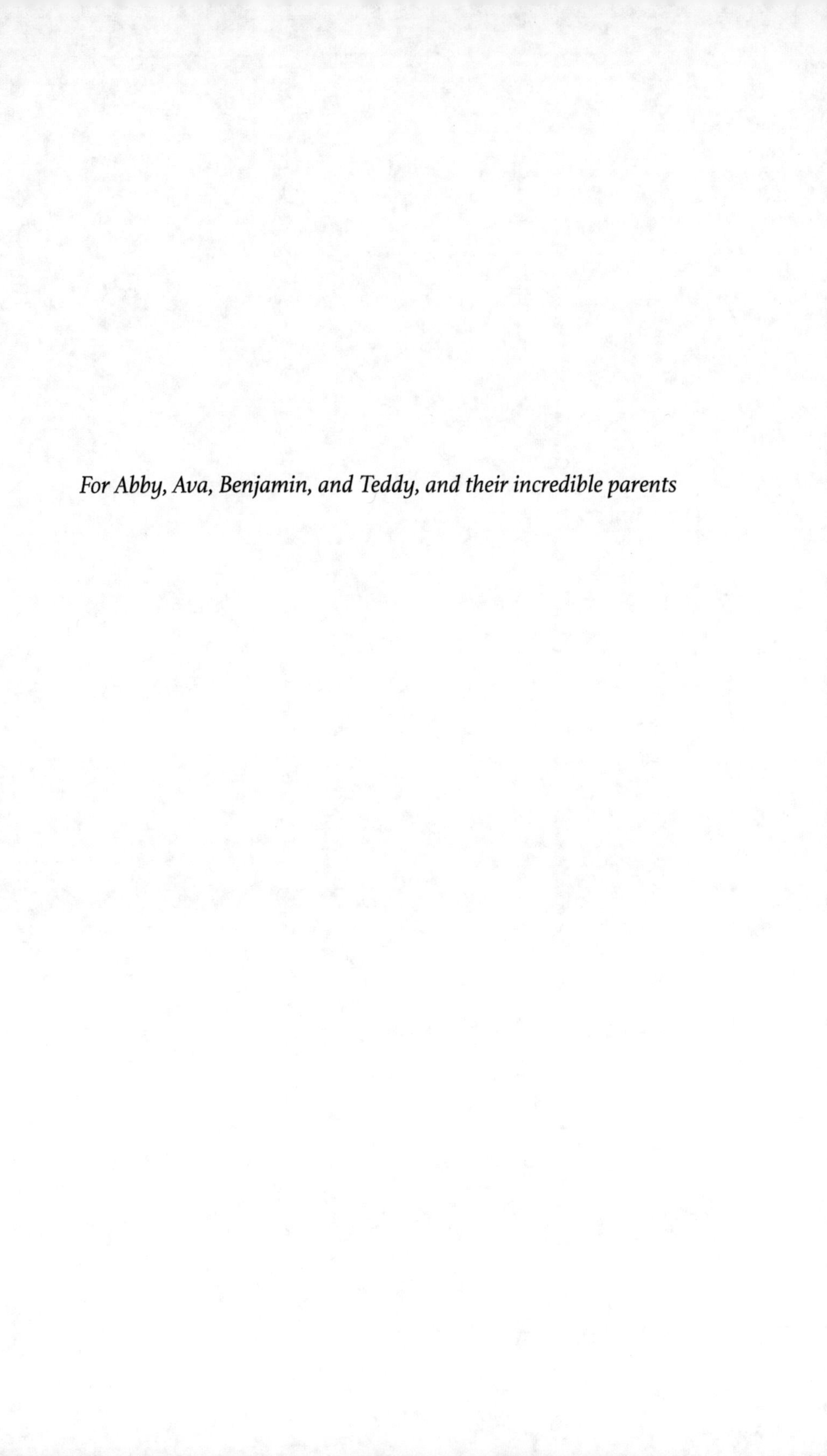

For Abby, Ava, Benjamin, and Teddy, and their incredible parents

CHAPTER 1

The cry of a hawk startled Leonora Morgan awake. As she wondered what prey had eluded the raptor, she stirred and turned to the clock. Then, with a sigh, she leaned back on the pillows to gaze at her husband still fast asleep. *As handsome as the day we met,* she thought, reaching over to smooth back his thick salt-and-pepper hair.

Their fortieth anniversary, the wedding of their son, Kyle, *and* Christmas were less than a week away, and she had a million things to do. She snuggled deeper into the mass of down pillows and let her mind drift back to a crisp fall day in California.

As she walked across campus with her dearest friend, Suzie Miller, they met Spark and Patsy Foster. Newlywed twenty-one-year-olds, Spark and Patsy had married a week earlier against the wishes of both of their families. Patsy came from money, Spark did not, but he was well on his way to making his fortune in alternative energy. An engineering major, the previous summer he had experimented with methanol, which had bombed. Now he was investing heavily in solar.

"Hey, ladies, glad we met you," Patsy said, smiling at Suzie, whom she knew well. Leonora had only met the perky redhead once. "We're having a small wedding celebration tomorrow night, and we'd love for you both to join us."

Alongside the newlyweds stood a tall, lanky young man with eyes the color of cornflowers and chestnut hair thick and tousled as if he'd just hopped out of bed. His eyes never left Leonora, a gentle, steady gaze that felt warm and comfortable. *Like the home I've had never had,* she mused.

"That sounds fun," Suzie said, smiling at her friend. "You remember Nora?"

"Sure we do," Patsy said, eyes twinkling as she gazed at Leonora. "And this is Spark's best friend, Ben Morgan."

"I've seen you," Suzie gushed, stepping forward to shake his hand. "Will you be at the party?"

"You bet," he replied, smiling at Suzie, then turning to Leonora. "Pleased to meet you, Nora."

As Ben Morgan shook her hand, Leonora's knees wobbled and she felt light-headed. His hand trembled as it grasped hers. When she looked up, she was startled to glimpse a depth of feeling in his eyes.

"Yes, hi, you too," she finally managed to sputter. *Drop-dead gorgeous, that's what he is.* Completely unlike any of the men she knew. Lanky and solid, Ben wore jeans, a collared dress shirt open at the neck, and scuffed cowboy boots. Different pair, but the same brand he still wore today. He towered over her at six feet six, as did his handsome best friend, Spark. Even as a young man, Spark was often mistaken for the actor Fred Thompson.

Ben shook her hand. Later, he told her that his first sight of her had hit him like a lightning bolt and he knew right then that he was looking at the woman with whom he would spend his life. About a foot shorter than him, she was slender, with full, rounded breasts. She wore a short pencil skirt and matching green cashmere sweater. *And oh those legs!*

"Please say you'll both come," Patsy said, squeezing her husband's arm. "It would mean so much to us."

"Of course we'll come, won't we, Nora?" Suzie said, looking from Patsy to her.

"Of course." Leonora nodded, afraid to look up into those blue eyes again.

~

Drawing her back from her remembering, Ben reached for her. "Hey, beautiful, good morning."

"Hey, yourself."

"Penny for your thoughts."

"Well, if you must know, I was thinking back to Stanford and the first time I set eyes on a certain handsome cowboy."

He chuckled. "Country bumpkin next to Ms. Bel Air Sophisticate."

"Yet you still managed to sweep me off my feet and carry me off to the valley you couldn't stop talkin' about."

"Desperate times require desperate measures. 'Sides, I was afraid if I stopped talking, you'd get bored and walk away. The Valley was the only topic I could say more than two syllables about."

"Well, we know that's not true. Desperate?"

"Couldn't imagine livin' another day without you."

"And, now here we are. Forty years later."

"Blink of an eye, darlin'. Wouldn't change a second."

"Nor would I," she said, smiling as she slid down beside him.

"That's more like it." He kissed her as he drew her into his arms.

"Mmm," she said. "Someone's perky this morning."

"Always."

After four decades, the elder Morgans were more in love with each other than ever, still learning what gave the other pleasure. This morning was no different as his gentle, rough hands moved under her satin night shirt to caress Leonora's magnificent, full breasts. As he trailed kisses from her lips, down her long slender neck, she unbuttoned her top and moved against him.

As her husband took one breast, then the other into his mouth, tongue circling, teasing her nipples, she murmured, "Oh, sweetie, you're still pushing all my buttons. Please, please, put me out of my misery." As she spoke, Leonora's hands caressed him, then slid his boxers down over his hips, casting them aside with her toes.

"Gladly," he said, gently parting her legs and entering her. *Home*, he sighed as they moved as one toward a tremulous, loving climax.

After, as they lay entwined, he kissed the tip of her nose and said the same words he uttered every time they made love. "Thanks, darlin'."

"You're welcome, cowboy," she said, responding as she always did.

"You ready for the big parties?"

"I'd rather stay here and snuggle with you," she said, settling into the crook of his shoulder.

"That's what I like to hear."

"But, there are lists a mile long, Ben. Are you sure we should be doing this along with Kyle and Harriet's wedding? I hate to steal their thunder."

"No danger of us ole fogies stealing thunder or anything else from those two young firecrackers, darlin'."

"I suppose not, but there's so much to do. Yikes, that list is long! Then there's the celebration for Gail and Tim and the rehearsal dinner! Not to mention Christmas! Thank goodness we decorated early. That's done, at least. I want everything to be super special."

"It will be. Vermillion'll do a great job with the party for Gail and Tim," he said, referring to a nearby farm-to-table restaurant. "And Friday night's a barbecue. Spark has Aria and her crew handling all that," he added, referring to their dear friend and his chef Aria Firorelli.

"I know, I know... That's what we should have said about our party: low key!"

He grinned, hand massaging her back. "How many people are comin' to this shindig?"

"About a hundred."

"Hmm...a little more than low key by Valley standards, but not too much for our crew."

"Ever the optimist." She kissed his cheek. "That's why I love you so much."

Instead of rising immediately, Leonora lay back down and snuggled against him.

"What's wrong, sweetheart?"

"I was just thinking back to what a snob I was."

"Never."

"Yes, I was. Awful."

"Don't remember any such thing."

"Yes, you do, because you were the one reining me in. Think how nasty I was about Maggie when Ben started dating her."

"You love your children, that's all."

"Oh, pish tush." She gave him a peck on the cheek as she moved away and sat up. "You have a blind spot where I'm concerned. Always have."

"Always will."

She smiled. "I love you, Ben Morgan."

"Right back at you, darlin'."

As she stood, Leonora grabbed the side table, faltering.

"That's it. We're gonna see the doc."

"It's just my pesky old knee."

"It's more than that, honey, and you know it. You used to love to ride, but you haven't gone near Misty for three years."

"Misty is busy enough with all the lessons and pony camps," she said, referring to her beautiful white Andalusian, an anniversary gift from her husband years ago.

"That's not the point, and you know it. You hurt, and I hurt for you."

"Let's talk about this later. Okay? I've got a million and one things to do." She leaned over, kissed his forehead, then disappeared into the bathroom, forestalling any further discussion.

CHAPTER 2

"You sure you're okay with this, babe?" Kyle asked as they settled in the plane for the trip west.

Harriet smiled. "What? Getting married?"

"Ha-ha. No, I meant with the wedding at the ranch and the whole triple event with my parents' anniversary and the celebration for Gail and Tim."

She leaned over and kissed him. "Of course I'm okay with it. Mom's keyed, and my sisters can't wait to see the Valley."

"I just don't want anything to steal your special day."

Her hand grazed his cheek, tracing a line along his firm, handsome jaw. "My special day happened the day we met. Now, if you're standing beside me, that's all that matters. You know I'm not much of a limelight person."

"You okay about your dad being there?"

Her face clouded, and Harriet frowned. "He wanted to come. I didn't feel I could say no."

"But I can. To protect you and your mom."

Harriet smiled at him, hand gently caressing his jawline. "It's okay, my champion. Mom's strong, and I've made my peace with it and Dad. As you know, my wicked stepmother is coming too, since she's *dying to see the Valley.*' She'll have to babysit him."

Kyle gazed at his fiancée, who rarely spoke harshly about anyone. He had only met her dad once, and the impression he took away was of a depressed, late-middle-aged dreamer. Rita had been traveling at the time, so he had not yet met Jud Morgan's second wife. "Where are they staying?"

"The Lodge," she said, referring to the large inn and spa on his parents' ranch, Morgan's Run. "They don't get in until Friday afternoon, thank goodness. And they'll be gone early Sunday."

"They the only ones at the Lodge?"

"No, Frankie's there. She can handle Dad and Rita. Most of Tim's family are at the Lodge. The only other Yarners coming are Tim's aunt Grace and Mavis, and they're there. My guess is Dad and Rita will be so intimidated by that crowd that they'll keep a low profile." The Darn Yarners, including Frankie Brown and Harriet's mom, Helen, were a group of dear friends from the village of Horseshoe Crab Cove, friends who had supported and loved each other for many years.

"Karen's with you at Spark's, right?"

"Yup. Remarkably, Spark's managed to fit Karen and most of my family since he has a million bedrooms. What about your friends? I have to admit I haven't been keeping up with the guest list."

Kyle smiled, reaching over to take her hand and squeezing it. "Why would you with my mother in charge? I only have a couple comin' from vet school and my college roommate, John. John's staying with Beth and Lang, and the two vet school buddies are at the Lodge too."

"It's gonna be fine, isn't it?" she asked as the plane took off.

"Course it is, babe." *If your father behaves.*

"SO WHAT CAN MAGGIE AND I DO?" BEN MORGAN ASKED. "KIDS ARE AT the Cottage right now and Mag's at the stables, but we can do airport runs, get food in. Anything you need."

His parents sat at the dining room table enjoying a late lunch.

"Thanks, honey," Leonora said. "I think we're set for now. Spark has ordered a fleet of cars for the week, and they'll be running to and from the airport. Between Aria and her crew and Carmela, the food is well in hand. Johnny arrives tomorrow, and he'll be a huge help." She referred to chef Johnny Stockdale, who ran the kitchen for Emma's Dream, the ranch's summer camp for handicapped children.

"Remind me who's staying with us," her son asked.

"Richard's daughter Ava and her family. Their children will have such fun with Emma and Bennie."

"We're excited. Who's here with you guys?" Her dark-haired, handsome son looked from one to the other.

"Just Kyle and Harriet, her sister Hazel, and Sam and Rose. We're holding out the last two bedrooms for stragglers," Ben Senior said. "We wish we could have everyone here."

"I can't wait to meet my next precious grandbaby," Leonora said.

"Maggie was surprised she's traveling now," her son said.

"Doctors have their own rules, I guess," Ben Senior replied. "Maybe she'll have a Valley baby."

"We'd sure love it." Leonora grasped the table as she rose on shaky legs.

"You okay, Mom?"

"Fine, fine. Just a little stiff."

Ben Senior observed her but said nothing.

His son stood. "Well, okay, then, I've gotta get movin'. I've got some errands in town, then I'll pick up the kids and head back to greet everyone."

"Dinner's at the Lodge tonight," his father said. "See you all later." When the door closed behind their son, he turned to his wife, who was stacking their lunch plates. "Okay, let's talk, darlin'."

"Didn't I tell you later?"

"This is later, and I can't sit by and watch you limping around. You wince every time you stand up."

Leonora waved her hand. "It's nothing. Just a funny range-of-motion issue. When all the festivities are over, I'll get it checked out."

Ben frowned. "I'd rather you do it now."

"Didn't slow me down this morning, did it?" She winked at him as she headed for the kitchen.

Ben followed her as she handed the lunch things to Carmela, their cook and housekeeper. "Can we talk about this Nora? I'm serious."

"Thanks, Carm," she said, leading the way to the back terrace, where she sat on a bench in the shade. She patted the seat beside her, and he sat down. "There's nothing to say. It's this," she said, raising her legs out straight in front of her. "I can't get them farther apart than this. That's why I can't get on a horse, and I wouldn't feel comfortable riding even if I managed to somehow hoist myself into the saddle."

"You haven't wanted to ride for at least a year."

"You were more accurate this morning. Three years."

"So this has been comin' on?"

She nodded.

"Why didn't you tell me?"

"I kept thinking it would get better. You know I do my stretching every morning and yoga."

"I'm gonna call Lang and get a recommendation for an orthopedic doc. Today. They interact with those fellas all the time through Rambler Sports."

"That's not necessary. Besides, I don't want the kids to know," she said, tears rimming her eyes.

"I'll ask Lang to keep it quiet."

"He'd better. Besides, I'm just getting old, that's all."

He reached over to envelop her in his strong arms. "Never, darlin'. You look as young as you did the day we met and even more beautiful."

Leonora smiled. "Then we'd better make an appointment for you to see an eye doctor."

"So do I have the go-ahead to call Lang?"

She nodded. "Okay, but hush, hush, hush. And no interfering with any of the party planning and events. Promise?"

"Promise," he said, kissing the tip of her nose. "I love you, Nora."

"Right back at you," she said, hugging him.

CHAPTER 3

Family and friends arrived throughout the day. Spark's fleet of limos was kept busy shuttling people from Grenville Airport. Wedding guests were staying everywhere. Bebe Corcoran, the assistant manager at the Lodge, had created a schedule that listed events for the next four days as well as a listing of guests and where they were staying. There were copies in all the Lodge guest rooms, and Bebe had dropped off copies at the Big House and Spark's. Each limo driver also had a stack to present to guests upon arrival.

Events
Wednesday, 6:30 p.m.: Dinner, at the Lodge at Morgan's Run
Thursday: All day by appointment, Trail Rides, Stables at Morgan's Run
Thursday, 7-10 p.m.: Celebration of Gail and Tim Miller's Nuptials,
Vermillion
Friday, 6:30-11 p.m., Rehearsal Dinner for Harriet and Kyle, Spark Foster's
Saturday 4 p.m.: Harriet & Kyle's Wedding, Saguaro Valley Chapel,
Reception at the Big House, Morgan's Run
Sunday, 3 p.m.: Ben and Leonora Morgan: A Celebration of 40 Years of
Marriage, The Lodge at Morgan's Run

"What a house," Tim said as he, Gail, and her three brothers stepped out of the limo at Harley and Ruthie's.

"Come on up," Harley called as he descended the steps of the front walkway, a toddler with red curls on his hip. "Ruthie's still at the farm, but she'll be home soon. Welcome." A tall thin young woman with straight flaxen hair walked by his side. "This is our daughter Willow, and this is Charlotte. Fortunately for them, they both take after their beautiful mothers." Pride shone in the handsome wrangler's eyes as he gazed from one daughter to the other.

"Hi," Willow said. "Can I help with your bags?"

Gail smiled at her. "Thanks, but with these four guys and your dad, I think we're all set."

They were ushered in and up to bedrooms, all with breathtaking views of the mountains and valley. Teddy and Ben were sharing a room, Rich a smaller room that also served as an office, and Gail and Tim a large room furnished with a rustic four-poster queen-size bed adorned with an exquisite patchwork quilt. The dresser and end tables were finished to match, and Navaho rugs in bright earth colors were scattered on the wide pine floors. "Come on down for a drink once you get settled," Harley said, leaving them to unpack.

"Wow, we're not in New England any more, are we?" Gail turned to her husband, arms circling his broad shoulders.

"Sure aren't, but this is pretty cool. Can't wait to explore."

"Think we dare go riding tomorrow?" she asked, nuzzling his neck.

Tim kissed her lightly. "I'm game if you are."

"Always. Now let's unpack and see the rest of this spectacular house."

ONE OF SPARK'S STRETCH LIMOS ARRIVED AT SIX TO PICK UP THE ADULTS at Harley and Ruthie's. Despite her father's protests, Willow had insisted on sitting for Charlotte. Even as they were walking out the door, he said, "The baby can come tonight, darlin'. Why don't you change your mind and come with us?"

Charlotte on her hip, Willow gave her father a gentle nudge. "Out you go. We'll be with you all weekend. Time for you guys to have a grown-up night."

Ruthie leaned over and hugged Willow, then kissed her toddler's chubby cheek. "She's right, Harley. Come on. Night, baby girl. You be good for Willow."

As they drove away, Gail said, "Your daughter's a lovely young woman. Baby's adorable too."

Harley grinned. "Yeah, they're pretty incredible. We're lucky."

"It's so great to have you all here," Ruthie said, gazing around at her cousins. Ben and Rich had dark hair like three of her brothers and Teddy, who bore a remarkable resemblance to her brother Robbie had sandy hair and light eyes. Gail's fiancé, Tim, was dark and gorgeous, every bit the image of Heathcliff, the nickname villagers used for him in Horseshoe Crab Cove. Gail was petite and freckle-faced very like Ruthie herself.

"Great to be here," Teddy said.

The others nodded.

"And we're looking forward to your shindig tomorrow night," Ruthie said.

Gail smiled. "We are too!"

"Unusual name, Vermillion," Tim said.

Harley nodded. "Named for the yellow soil all around the farm. It's a cool place. Owners are real nice people. Food's spectacular."

"I thought vermillion was a blood-red color," Teddy said.

Harley grinned. "You're not the first artist who's pointed that out. Apparently, there are various shades of vermillion. Maybe we should split the difference and call it orange."

Ruthie rolled her eyes. "Maybe we should talk about something more interesting like what you want to do while you're here. There's great hiking, riding, of course, exploring around town. Beth and I would love to give you a tour of the farm." The two sisters ran the ranch's huge organic farm on the western edge of Morgan's Run.

"Tim and I were just talking about riding," Gail said.

"Ask Maggie tonight. They'll set you up. I bet they could find someone to take you out for a trail ride."

"Love to take a hike or two," Teddy said.

"Count me in," Rich said.

"Talk to my brother Robbie," Ruthie said. "He might even go with you. He's just started an outdoor adventure business in town. They mostly take people rafting, but they lead hikes too. I wish I didn't have to work, or I'd be out there hiking or riding."

"Well, I'd love a tour of the farm," Ben said, "So I'm happy to take you up on that."

IF THE BIG HOUSE WAS HOMEY WITH CHRISTMAS IN EVERY ROOM, ON every surface, the Lodge was magical. Jim Thompson and his staff had outdone themselves with decorations collected over many years. Greenery with red berries, bows, and baubles trimmed every available spot, twinkle lights everywhere.

"Oh my goodness!" Rachel Miller said as she and her sister Karen greeted Maggie Morgan. "I've never seen decorations like this!"

"Never mind the decorations," Karen said. "Look at them!" She eyed the Morgan brothers, Ben, Sam, Kyle, and Robbie, who stood near the door of the Lodge greeting people. "I've never seen so many gorgeous men in one place, and they're all attached or married!"

Maggie laughed. "That group, maybe, but not the eastern cousins. Rich, Teddy, and cousin Ben are pretty cute and all unattached, I believe?"

Karen frowned. "Yes, but they're not cowboys."

"Neither are Sam and Kyle anymore," Maggie said, eyes widening as her son Ben ran by. "I knew we should have gotten a sitter. Would you excuse me, Karen?"

"Of course. Do you need help?"

"I've got it, thanks. Enjoy yourself."

Across the room, the brothers stood together as the last of the guests trickled in. "What's with Mom?" Kyle asked, directing his remarks to Ben. Ben was the oldest Morgan offspring. He and Robbie both lived in the Valley.

Ben frowned. "Whaddya mean? She's in her usual form, orderin' everyone around, into everyone's business."

"That's just it. She isn't. She's been clinging to Dad all night, and she looks frail to me."

Robbie nodded. "That's 'cause she is."

"What?" Ben said.

"Haven't you noticed her limping around?"

Ben shook his head. "I mean, they both do that. Now that you mention it, she was kind of tottery this morning."

"And she doesn't ride anymore," Robbie said.

"That's nothing new. She hasn't taken Misty out for years."

"Ever wonder why? She and Dad used to love riding."

"Well, brothers," Sam said. "I hate to say this, but our parents aren't getting any younger. There's Dad's heart. Maybe Mom has a little arthritis."

"I'm gonna ask Dad," Kyle said.

Ben scratched his head, gazing across the room to where Maggie was wrestling with their son. "I'd leave it alone. That's my advice, bro. I'd better go rescue Maggie. Geez, Mags was right. We should've gotten a sitter."

They had closed the Lodge to outside guests for the weekend, so the terrace and dining areas were theirs. Tables were set with brightly colored linens and pottery. Ben and Leonora sat with his brother Richard and his wife, Lucy, as well as Spark and Helen, Lucy's mother. "As usual, George has outdone himself," Spark said, referring to George Baran, the inn's head chef.

Ben Senior smiled, gazing over at his brother and Lucy. "Everything we're eating was raised here on the ranch. Pork's from the farm, humanely raised and slaughtered, and our two girls grew and harvested the vegetables."

"Not single-handedly," his wife said.

Ben winked. "And we have a baker who comes to the Lodge three days a week. She makes all the breads and most of the desserts. Not sure what George has planned for dessert, but it'll be good. Yep, everything Valley raised including the wine. That's from down the road."

"Excellent wines," Richard said. "Are the Dillons here?" He referred to Jaybo and Martha Dillon, owners of Saguaro Vineyards and parents of Lang Dillon, Beth Morgan's husband, and Rose Dillon Morgan, wife of Sam Morgan.

"Not tonight," Leonora said. "They'll be here for the wedding and our party Sunday, but he's not too well, so they pick and choose what to attend. Too bad for Martha. She loves a good party, but she won't leave him. Maybe the kids can persuade her to come tomorrow or Friday."

Richard nodded. "Well, I look forward to seeing them to thank them for their hospitality with our Wolfie. They gave him so much information and such valuable contacts."

"Jaybo knows his stuff," Ben Senior said, reaching under the table to squeeze his wife's hand.

As the evening ended and the cousins poured into limos, Range Rovers, and trucks, Leonora and Ben stood at the Lodge entrance, his arm around her. "Great party, baby," he said, kissing the top of her head.

"Back at ya," she said, leaning into him.

"Ready to go home?"

"Absolutely, and here's our ride now," she said as Sam and Rose drove up in his father's Escalade, the others following in Leonora's Volvo. Sam and Rose were staying at the Big House along with Kyle and Harriet and her sister Hazel.

CHAPTER 4

The next morning, the younger generation dispersed to a number of activities. Spark offered to take Rex and Faith Miller, along with her sister Grace, on a tour of the Valley to include lunch at Valley Stables. Aria packed a huge basket of food, and the group set off. Helen stayed behind and went with Ava, her children, Rich, and Maggie for a tour of the farm and Morgan's Run stables, with the promise of a horseback ride. Dan Fielding, Ava's husband, joined a number of the guys for a hike, and Gail and Tim met Harriet and Kyle at the stables for a trail ride. Nick Parker had horses saddled for them as well as Karen and Rachel Miller and Weezie Morgan.

Nick stood watching the group as they mounted up. "Careful on the ascent if you're taking the east trail. There's been a lot of loose rock after the rain."

"Thanks, Nick," Kyle said, patting Royal, his dad's horse. "You here alone today?"

"Naw. Jeb'll be in later and we have a new guy, Kenny. He should be here when you get back. Have a good ride."

"Yet another gorgeous cowboy." Karen sighed, gazing at Rachel. "I wonder if he'll be at the wedding."

Karen was riding Rowdy, Ben Junior's quarter horse. Harriet

overheard her remark and smiled, deciding it was best not to tell Karen that Nick was gay.

~

"WHAT ARE YOUR PLANS FOR TODAY, HONEY?" LEONORA ASKED, directing her remarks to her son Sam. Sam, Ben Senior, and she sat at the breakfast table, sipping coffee.

"I'm waiting to see how Rosie feels. We'll probably go over to her parents' for a while, then maybe take a drive. We want to see all the improvements out at Valley Stables."

His mother nodded. "You'll be amazed. Galahad, the newest thoroughbred, is gorgeous. Quite the prettiest horse I've ever seen."

"Handsomest, darlin'," her husband said. "Don't go callin' a stud like Galahad pretty."

Leonora waved her hand. "Oh pish tush." She gazed up, spying Rose in the doorway. "Here she is. Mornin', honey. How you doin'?"

One hand on her large, pregnant belly, her daughter-in-law gave her a wan smile. "Honestly, I've been better, but I will say our bed has the most comfortable mattress I've ever slept on. Is it new?"

Leonora smiled. "We make it a point to change all the mattresses every ten years, but the secret to that one is the topper."

"Well, whatever it is, I wish we could take it home with us," Rose said, helping herself to a slice of toast from the sideboard.

"We could have one shipped right to your door, honey. Be waiting when you and Sammy get home."

"Thanks, but I daresay I'll survive."

Sam hopped up to take her plate. "Want tea, sweetheart?"

She smiled at him. "That would be great."

"What else could Carmela fix you, honey?" Leonora asked, noticing the one slice of toast.

Rose eased herself into a chair. "Nothing right now, thanks. Let's see how this settles."

"Have you talked to your folks this morning?" Ben Senior asked.

"Not yet. We're going to stop in, check on things, and maybe persuade Mom to come out with us. She's like a prisoner over there."

Leonora nodded. "Yes, poor dear. I miss her terribly. She hasn't been to Cowbelles in months." She referred to the charity organization to which most Valley women belonged.

"I'm going to talk to my brother," Rose said. "This can't go on. She needs help."

"Didn't they have someone?" Leonora asked.

"Yes, and Dad fired her. It doesn't help that Lang and my dad are like oil and water so that when he tries to intervene, there's usually a huge blowup and Mother begs him to back off. But it's time to try again. It's not fair to her."

"Well, if there's anything we can do, just holler," Ben said.

"Thanks." Rose reached over to pat her father-in-law's hand. "You do plenty. Just staying with you is huge. I love my parents, but it's so much more relaxing over here."

"Well, if you change your mind," Leonora said, "your room and that mattress are yours as long as you're here. And we can have the men take the mattress and topper to your parents' house, if that will help you be more comfortable."

Rose smiled as Lang returned and set the tea in front of her. His parents rose.

"We have an appointment in town," Ben said. "Be back in the early afternoon."

As they drove the twenty-five miles to orthopedist's office at Valley Hospital, Leonora turned to him. "Why did you tell the kids our appointment was in town?"

He turned to her, eyes soft. "Didn't think you wanted to worry them."

"Well, you were right. Are you worried?"

"Nope."

"Why not?"

"'Cause we're gonna see this hotshot sports doc. I'm sure he'll fix you right up."

Leonora leaned over, head on his shoulder. "Always the optimist. That's why I fell in love with you, Ben Morgan."

"Darn these bucket seats or I could scooch you right up to me."

Leonora laughed. "Bucket seats! You're dating yourself now, cowboy. We haven't had bucket seats since your old Mustang."

They parked in the shade and held hands as they headed into the clinic building attached to the back of the hospital. Dr. Edgemore's office was on the first floor. The waiting room was nearly empty when they stepped in, with only one couple sitting near the door. As the Morgans took their seats, clipboard of forms in hand, the other couple was called in. Fifteen minutes later, it was their turn.

Dr. Edgemore's PA, Joseph, took Leonora's vitals and they were soon joined by the doctor himself. Tall and slender, he had freckles and bright red curly hair cut short. Joseph, who appeared to be in his twenties, could pass for his boss's son. "Hey, folks. Phil Edgemore, good to meet you." He extended his hand, which each of them shook in turn. "What brings you in to see me?"

Ben said, "Our son-in-law, Lang Dillon, recommended you because my wife's been having some pain and range-of-motion issues in both legs. We wondered about exercises for her knees."

"Lang's a great guy. His Rambler Sports sells some of the best equipment in the business. I'm always referring clients to him for hiking shoes."

Ben nodded. "Yup, Lang's a keeper for sure."

Dr. Edgemore turned to Leonora and smiled. "Now, Mrs. Morgan, can I ask you to hop up on the table so I can examine your legs?"

"Silly me, I wore a skirt," she said, indicating one of her signature lime-green skorts.

"No worries. I'll be discreet. Just want to check your knees." Gently, he manipulated both knees and legs, asking about pain or discomfort. When he completed his examination, he said, "I'd like to get some X-rays of your knees and hips. Would that be okay?"

Leonora frowned. "Is that *really* necessary?"

"I think it would be prudent. Your movements are very restricted for a sixty-three-year-old. I'm surprised you aren't in more pain."

Arms folded across her chest, she said, "Fine. Let's do it."

CHAPTER 5

"Hey, darlin', no need for that," Ben said, looking up from his menu to spy tears snaking down his beautiful wife's cheeks. They'd decided to swing by their club and have lunch after leaving Dr. Edgemore's office. At a table in a secluded nook on the club terrace, they were almost invisible to their fellow diners.

"No need for me anymore either," Leonora sniffed. "I'm old and broken. Might as well go to bed now and stay there."

He smiled, patting her hand. "I'd love to hop into bed with you and stay there forever."

"Pish tush! Don't be silly!"

He grinned, a mischievous gleam in his blue eyes. "And your bum hip doesn't seem to be bothered in that department. You're still as sexy as ever."

Leonora leaned forward whispering. "It's actually when it feels best. Relaxed and warm. It's the rest of our life where I'm a useless old hag."

"Never. We're gonna have you fit as a fiddle in no time. 'Sides, who'd look after me and all my ailments if you hide in bed? You forget about my creaky old heart."

"No, I don't. That's just it! I can't fall apart. Forget it. I'll live with the aches and pains. I can't be laid up or using a walker. Too much to do!"

"Did you hear Dr. Edgemore? In your shape, you'll make a quick recovery."

Leonora wiped her eyes with her napkin as the waitress approached. "Hello, Betsy. I'm gonna have the field greens salad with grilled salmon, and he'll have the same. Two iced teas, thanks." She grabbed Ben's menu and handed both to Betsy.

Betsy nodded. "Be right back with your teas."

"What if I wanted a Rueben?" he asked.

"Did you?"

"Kind of."

"Okay, then let's get her back."

Leonora hopped up, tossing her napkin down. He reached forward and grabbed her arm. "The salad's fine, honey. Sit down."

Leonora plunked down, a movement she did more frequently due to the stiffness in her legs. "Fine."

"Listen to me, honey. The hip replacement's an option. We'll contact folks we know who've had them and see what they say. Then you can make your decision."

"How will I tell the kids? How can I face them?"

"Same way you do every day. We can tell 'em together once we get all the facts."

Leonora nodded as Betsy set down their teas and hurried away. "Not now! Not until after the holidays."

"Whatever you want. Now who do you know who's had a hip replacement? That's where to begin. I'll do some quiet checking too."

"A few of the Cowbelles have had them. Helen Winthrop too."

"Harriet's mom?"

Leonora nodded. "She told me about it last year. She has pretty painful arthritis in winter too."

"Well, there you go. Look how she gets around."

A small smile crept over his wife's face. "What would I do without my Mr. Pollyanna?"

"That's the spirit!" He raised his tea in a toast. "To my beautiful bride, who I love more every minute of every day."

"Right back atcha, husband of mine. Love you more." She smiled, clinking her glass against his, tears rimming her green eyes.

"Wish I could order a big ole rainbow right over you, Nora Morgan!"

"What was Mom and Dad's appointment about?" Ruthie asked as she and Beth waited for the cousins to come for a tour of the farm.

"Not sure. Dad asked Lang about orthopedic doctors the other day. He knows Lang sees Phil Edgemore every five minutes for one of his running injuries, and Phil also recommends some of Rambler's products to his patients." Lang Dillon ran a very successful online sporting goods company. The first store had opened in Boston, then Rambler Sports West when he moved to the Valley.

"Hope Dad's okay," Ruthie said. 'I'm gonna check with Mom later."

Beth nodded as two large SUVs came up the drive and parked. "The cousins have arrived."

"Hi, guys!" Ruthie called as Ava and her children tumbled out of one vehicle along with Willow, Rich Morgan, and Ruthie's daughter, Charlotte. Harriet's sister Clara, her husband, Will, and their teenagers, Punky and Will Junior, as well as Lucy's kids, Amy and Rob, hopped out of the other. "Wow, we've got all ages. This is great! Why don't you older kids decide who'd like to drive the three golf carts, and we'll head out to see the animals first."

"This is amazing," Will said as he held Laura, their two-year-old, on top of the fence watching a herd of cattle in the westernmost pasture. The kids were not far off, crowded around Raoul, the livestock manager, who was showing off a new litter of piglets. "Hard to believe it's Arizona. You imagine it's all desert or forest in the north. This lush green is so unexpected."

Beth smiled. "Has anyone explained the orographic effect that created the cloud cover and humidity in this valley? There are books on it, if you're interested. It has to do with air flow between the mountains. We're very fortunate. Without it, we'd never be able to grow and raise what we do."

"My dad told us this is the largest organic farm in the southwest," Ava said.

Beth smiled. "One of them. My grandfather and then our dad knew what they were doing when they bought up all this land."

"It's beautiful," Ava said. "By the way, your sister's great with the kids," she added, watching her cousin chasing Sasha, Cameron, and Charlotte around the pigpen, Clara observing.

Beth grinned. "Yes, she loves every minute."

"Where's your Lily today?" Ava asked.

"With my mother-in-law. Lang's mom doesn't get out much, but she loves babysitting. Ordinarily, Lily would be at the Cottage. That's the day care my parents and Spark started on the ranch. But it's closed till after Christmas to give Polly and her coworkers a break."

"I've heard so much about that," Ava said. "You're so lucky. I'd love to see it."

"I'm sure my mom would love to give you a tour. It's her baby, even though the credit really belongs to Lynn and Polly, who set it up in the first place."

Clara strolled over and joined them at the fence. "Okay, sweetie," she said, patting Will's shoulder. "I'm ready to move out here. What about you?"

CHAPTER 6

Lights twinkled along the roofline of Vermillion's barn as guests arrived in the twilight. While the party for Tim and Gail was for family and close friends, it still required taking over the farm-to-table restaurant. Leonora had made all the arrangements after consulting with Gail, Tim, and their families. The menu featured local produce and cheeses, fish caught in nearby mountain streams, and Saguaro Valley wines. Grilled trout, luscious corn chowder, field greens, artisan cheese platters, roasted vegetables and desserts made with fresh local berries and fruits made up the simple six-course dinner with Saguaro Winery wines paired with each course.

Owner Edna Loggins bustled about directing her crew, which included her daughter, Nancy, and several other waiters. Their chef, Frances Bissett, manned the kitchen and Oscar, Edna's husband, was on hand to help with parking. He then came inside and tended bar.

"We don't have places like this at home," Richard Morgan said as he and Lucy strolled in with his family and her two teenagers, Amy and Rob, along with Spark and Buck Foster, the latter's son from Los Angeles. "Hmm... maybe with the vineyard, this might be a future kind of venture for our farm?"

Apple-cheeked Edna smiled, stepping aside as they entered. "Welcome! Enjoy every minute!"

"Hello, hello," Maggie Morgan said, strolling in beside a tall sixty-something man. "You all remember my dad, Ned Williams?"

They shook hands and stood chatting as other guests passed by. "Where's your handsome husband?" Lucy asked as she noticed her daughter Amy's eyes scanning the room.

Maggie laughed. "He's chasing our son, where else? They'll be in soon. Emma and Ben love to say hello to the animals out back. You look pretty tonight Amy. I love your blouse."

Lucy's fifteen-year-old blushed, fingering the hem of her gauzy cotton top, a lovely jade green that brought out the blue in her eyes. "Thanks. I got it this afternoon at Gabriela's. I love that place."

"Me too," Maggie said. "Even if my pocketbook doesn't. Gabriela's a genius at matching clothes to people. That color really suits you. We're so glad to have you back with us. She was our star counselor last summer. We hope she'll agree to come back next year," she added, directing her remarks to Lucy and Richard.

"I'd love to," Amy said. "And bring along a couple of my friends. They're dying to see the Valley." As she spoke, her eyes continued to dart around the dining room.

Maggie winked at Lucy. "Tommy's coming to the wedding. Some of the other counselors too. I'm sure they'll be excited to see you."

Amy's face fell. "Oh, not tonight, then?"

Maggie smiled. "This is mostly family and people who know Gail and Tim. Tomorrow night's also family and all about Kyle and Harriet. Saturday, however, the sky's the limit! Everyone will be there. Then there's my in-laws' anniversary party Sunday, so you'll have plenty of time to catch up."

Having observed the exchange, Buck Foster stepped forward. "Come on, Amy and Rob. Care to hit the bar with this old guy?" Thirty-three, with sandy hair and blue eyes, Spark's attractive, charming son held out his arm to Amy, who blushed as she took it.

"You don't think he'll get them something alcoholic, do you, Spark?" Lucy asked.

Their host chuckled. "Naw, unless he slips 'em one Desert Amber," he said, referring to the locally brewed beer.

"Oh, you think so? This is a busy weekend. I'd hate to see them crash and burn before it starts."

Richard put his arm around his wife. "We'll keep an eye on them, won't we, Spark?"

~

"Happy, wife of mine?" Tim asked as they stood together at Vermillion's entrance. They'd been at the door greeting people, but it now appeared that most guests had arrived. The cocktail hour was in full swing. At Leonora's request, Oscar had created a signature drink, G & T twist, a white wine spritzer with a sprig of mint.

Gail smiled up at him. "Honestly? I'm a little sore from our ride and never comfortable as the center of attention. Otherwise, I am blissfully happy. I love it here. And I love this spritzer thing. Mint! Who'd have thought?"

Tim kissed the top of her head. "I'll stick with the Desert Amber."

Gail gazed across the room, spying Jonas Miller talking to a beautiful raven-haired woman. "I see your brother's met Aria," she said, referring to Aria Firorelli, Spark's chef.

Tim grinned. "That's Jonas. Master of the impossible romance. He always hooks up with women who are inaccessible in some way or another."

Gail leaned against her husband, arm around his waist. "Well, I know one thing. Spark would skin him alive if he tried to lure Aria east."

"I wouldn't worry too much. Jonas is a love-'em-and-leave-'em type. A weekend fling is about as much commitment as he's likely to make to any woman."

"Poor Aria."

"Maybe she's the same way."

Gail rolled her eyes. "Spoken like a true love-'em-and-leave-'em type."

"Ha-ha."

"Great party," Jonas Miller said. "I'm Jonas, the groom's brother." He extended his hand to the beautiful dark-haired chef with intense violet eyes. Aria was all curves in a long-sleeved red dress that hugged her waist, its short flared skirt flouncy and flirty. The dress's most outstanding feature was its deep vee neck that offered a tantalizing peek at her magnificent cleavage.

"Just got better. I'm Aria, Spark's chef."

"Lucky Spark. Did you grow up here?"

She laughed, batting her eyelashes at Tim Miller's slender dark-haired brother with his piercing gray-blue eyes. "Hardly. I'm from Portland, Oregon. I've been cooking for Spark since I graduated from culinary school. In the beginning, I did his corporate catering, but after his wife, Patsy, died, I became his personal chef. When he moved here, so did I. Not sure the Valley will be my life, but I love Spark, and he makes the kinds of offers you can't refuse."

"Sounds like he's pretty successful."

She nodded. "His companies are some of the top, if not *the* top, companies in alternative energy all over the world."

"So I hear."

"What do you do?" she asked as they strolled toward the bar.

"Engineer. I work for a company called Raytheon. Pretty good company. Work's interesting, and I travel a lot."

"Lucky you."

From across the room, Kyle and Harriet held hands watching Aria and Jonas. "Oh, how nice for Aria," she whispered.

"You've always had a soft spot for Whip Woman," he said.

Harriet elbowed him. "Stop it. She's a real sweetie once you get to know her."

Kyle rolled his eyes. "Yeah, right. You forget that before I met you, she was on the prowl and I was prey."

"All a façade," Harriet said. "Now come on, I can see they want us to sit down for dinner."

ON THAT BLUSTERY DAY OVER FORTY YEARS AGO, BEN THOUGHT Leonora Brooks the most sophisticated woman he'd ever seen. As soon as he and his best friend were alone, the normally taciturn rancher had peppered Spark with questions. A wide grin on his face, his friend had replied, "So the mighty oak has fallen. I've been waitin' four years for this, buddy."

"Ha-ha. So what about Ms. Brooks from Bel Air?"

"Well, her dad's some bigshot Hollywood agent, Tom Brooks. Her mother, Lily, appears regularly in the society pages."

"So they wouldn't be too happy if she brought home a country bumpkin like me?"

"You just met the gal, Morgan. Give it time. You might hate her at your next encounter."

Ben shook his head. "She's the one, Spark. No doubt about it."

"She is a cutie-pie, that's for sure. Patsy's crazy about her. I think she's studyin' to be an interior designer."

"Another strike against me. My skills there are limited to what brand of woodstove to order for the cabin."

"We're on our way, buddy. You'll be a big-time rancher before you know it. You can hire her to decorate your big fancy house."

Ben laughed. "Let's see how we do at your party first."

CHAPTER 7

"Morning, honey. You look a million miles away," Leonora said, kissing the top of her husband's head. "And you sneaked out of bed early on me."

"Sorry, darlin'. I promised to take my brother and Lucy for a short trail ride, and we figured we'd better do it early before all hell breaks loose. Wanna meet up in town for lunch later?"

"Perfect. Text me when you're back. So where were you when I came in?" she said.

He grinned. "Thinkin' back to our courtship days."

"Oh Lord! Whirlwind romance, more like it." She hugged him round his strong shoulders.

Ben patted her hands. "Wish I didn't have to run."

"Off you go now, scoot! I've got a million things to do anyway."

Leonora headed to the kitchen as Ben scooped up the truck keys from the front hall table. After chatting with Carmela, she grabbed toast and a hard-boiled egg from the sideboard and poured a cup of coffee. Her notebook with all its lists sat beside her. As she munched her toast, she too thought back over forty years to those heady days.

~

THE MINUTE BEN MORGAN STEPPED INTO PATSY AND SPARK'S apartment, he had her in his sights and she him. Every time she glanced in his direction, she met his eyes, those blue eyes that touched her soul. Slowly, he inched his way across the room until he finally stood at her side. "Evenin', Ms. Brooks."

Leonora pretended to be startled, but in truth, she had surreptitiously observed every step of his journey across the crowded room. "Why, Mr. Morgan, how nice to see you again. And it's Leonora."

Then he smiled. That smile that still made her go weak at the knees after forty years of marriage. "It's Ben."

Before long, they had managed to slip out onto the apartment's tiny balcony porch, where they talked for hours about their studies, their hopes and dreams for the future, and a bit about their families. At the end of the night, he said, "Would you have dinner with me tomorrow night?"

From then on, they were inseparable. One evening, as they walked back to her apartment arm in arm, he said, "This might seem bold, but I'd love for you to see my valley. Would you come away for the weekend with me?"

Leonora stopped and stared up at him. "But we haven't... I mean, it's not that I don't want to, but—"

"No funny business," he said. "You can have your own room. I just want to show you the Valley."

Leonora stood on tiptoes, arms circling his neck. "You do make me smile. You have to know by now that I'd follow you to the ends of the earth, funny business or not. I'd love to see your valley."

Ben scooped her up, swinging her around in his arms. "Yippee!"

CHAPTER 8

Friday afternoon, Leonora drove to Grenville Airport to pick up her dear college friend, Suzie Miller. Ben had offered to go with her, but she wanted him at the Lodge to support Harriet and Kyle when her father arrived. Midafternoon, he and Spark sat on the Inn's shady terrace, chatting with the couple.

"You two don't have to stay," Harriet said, smiling at her soon-to-be father in law, whom she considered more of a father than the man for whom they waited. "I'm sure between Kyle and me, we can handle my father."

Ben hugged her. "I want to be here, darlin'. Wouldn't miss meeting your daddy for all the world."

"I know where your sons get the Morgan charm. Thank you."

"If you think the welcoming party's too big, I can make myself scarce," Spark said.

"It's just right," Harriet said. "And, if I'm not mistaken, here they come."

One of Spark's huge SUVs drove by the terrace and pulled up in front of the Lodge. The four of them rose and walked down the terrace steps and around to the front entrance just as a tall, heavyset man emerged from the SUV. His complexion was ruddy, and his sandy hair was thinning and flecked with gray. On the opposite side of the vehicle, the driver held the door for a redhead, who was talking a mile a minute.

Harriet stepped forward, Kyle right behind her, and embraced her father. "Hi, Dad."

Jud Winthrop's blue eyes were clouded as he reached out to his daughter. "Hey, honey," he said softly.

Harriet stepped back and grabbed Kyle's hand. "This is Kyle, my fiancé."

At six-four, Jud Winthrop was somewhat stooped, but he pulled himself straighter and reached out to grasp Kyle's hand in a firm shake. "Pleased to meet you, son. You're a lucky man."

"Thank you, sir. Don't I know it."

Tears sprang to Harriet's eyes as she watched Kyle interact with her father.

After a glance at his soon-to-be daughter-in-law, Ben Senior stepped forward, hand outstretched. "Welcome to the Valley, folks. I'm Kyle's dad."

Jud smiled, turning to him. "And the owner of this beautiful property, I understand."

"Somethin' like that," his host said, turning to his best friend. "This is Spark Foster, host of tonight's gathering and my dearest friend."

As Spark shook his hand, Rita Winthrop interrupted. "Well, if this isn't a group of handsome cowboys! And what a place! I can't wait to see more. Juddie and I stopped in Phoenix years ago but never saw anything like this. So green and glorious." Her bright red shoulder-length hair stuck up at odd angles as if she'd been sleeping on it for many hours.

"That's the orographic effect, darlin'," Spark said, grabbing her up in a bear hug, his de facto greeting for most newcomers. "We can explain all about it after you get settled in."

"I'll be waiting with bated breath." After hugging Harriet and Kyle, with air kisses all around, Rita took her husband's arm. "Come on, Juddie, let's head inside."

"Guess we're in charge of the bags," Kyle whispered to Harriet, who was pale as a ghost. For the hundredth time, he hoped they hadn't made a mistake inviting Jud and Rita Winthrop.

His father winked. "We'll get the kids to take 'em up. Come on, you two." He followed the Winthrops into the Lodge lobby.

"Driver can help too," Spark said, following the group.

Bebe Corcoran, the Inn's assistant manager, was manning the desk as the guests approached.

"Now you must tell us the schedule," Rita was saying to Ben as the others approached.

"It's all in your welcome packet, Mrs. Winthrop," Bebe said, passing a brightly colored bag to Rita.

"Dinner tonight is at six thirty, and tomorrow is completely open until the wedding at four thirty," Ben said. "We have a couple of my wife's dear friends and fellow Cowbelles on hand to give tours of the ranch, town, and our stables just north of here."

"Cowbelles?" Rita said.

Ben grinned. "Local women's group. They're active in local charitable events and activities. There'll be a couple of Spark's hired vehicles ready to take people around in the morning. Just let Bebe know what you'd like to do, and she can arrange it. Maybe a drive, then a nice lunch on the terrace here? Or a picnic out at the stables?"

"Sounds perfect, doesn't it, Juddie?"

He nodded, looking vaguely disoriented.

Harriet approached the desk and said, "I'm sure it's been a long day with flights and all. We'll let you two settle in."

"Thanks, dearie!" Rita said, waving dismissively. "Can't wait to see our rooms."

Bebe nodded. "Of course. Neil will take you up. He's one of our waiters and also a jack-of-all-trades here at the Lodge. I'll have the porter follow with your bags." She punched a bell and a slight blond young man approached and took the keys from her.

"Right this way, folks," he said.

Jud turned to his daughter. "See you later, then."

"Of course." Harriet leaned forward to kiss his cheek.

"Toodle-loo!" Rita said, waving over her shoulder, arm linked in Neil's.

"Can't say as I've ever seen hair quite that color before," Spark whispered as the elevator door closed on the threesome.

Despite her distress, Harriet laughed. "That's Rita's trademark. Clara's kids call her Ronald McDonald, and the color gets closer to his every year."

Ben put his arm around her shoulders. "Leonora's Cowbelles'll keep 'em busy, honey. Don't you give it another thought."

Harriet leaned against him, deriving comfort from his strength and love. "Thanks, Dad," she whispered.

Kyle heard her and smiled, grateful as always for his incredible family.

Spark nodded, clapping him on the back. "That's right. We'll keep her so busy, she won't know what hit her or her red hair."

As the group walked out of the Lodge to go their separate ways, a tall woman with wild salt-and-pepper hair and piercing blue eyes stepped out of another of Spark's fleet. Frankie Brown, one of Helen Winthrop's dearest friends and a fellow Darn Yarner, had been there since Wednesday and was thoroughly enjoying the Valley. "Hey," she called, eyes on Harriet.

"They've arrived," Harriet said, rolling her eyes as she exchanged looks with the woman she considered an aunt.

Frankie looked from Harriet to Kyle, then his father and Spark. "How'd it go?"

Harriet raised her hands. "Fine. It went fine and it's over."

"Only two days," Frankie said, patting her hand. "And not to worry. Between the Millers and me, we'll corral them and get them to Spark's in one piece."

"Thanks, Frankie. I hope they don't cause a ruckus," Harriet said, holding Kyle's hand in a tight grasp.

Frankie grinned. "No chance of that. Jud's always been afraid of me, and she's downright petrified."

Harriet smiled. "That's our Frankie. What have you been up to all day?"

"Well, your mom gave me the grand tour. If I didn't love Horseshoe Crab Cove so much, I'd move out here in a heartbeat." She turned to Kyle and his dad. "Your daughter-in-law, Hope Seymour, is a major talent, isn't she?"

"Sure is," Ben said proudly.

"Bought one of her paintings at that SD place in town. We got lost in there for hours this morning." She referred to Saguaro Dreams, a three-story emporium that was part art gallery, part gift shop, part clothing store and everything in between.

"How's Mom? I've barely seen her," Harriet asked.

"Fine, baby. Just fine. Your mom's stronger than all of us, and judging by the crowds the last two nights, she may not even have to bump into Jud and Bozo."

Harriet hugged Frankie. "I hope so. See you tonight."

"Can't wait." Frankie nodded to the three men who had stood back, quietly observing the exchange.

CHAPTER 9

I
t was almost five. Ben and Leonora lay on their king-size bed. Her list completed, she was half asleep, nestled in the crook of his arm. Ben smiled, looking over at her, grateful to his dear friend for hosting this evening's party. With Spark and Aria in charge, it meant that his Nora could rest. And she needed the rest. She had tried to cover it up, but when she returned from her errands, she was limping, favoring her sore hip. By the end of the weekend, she'd be a hurting cowgirl.

As he held her, he thought back to their first trip to the Valley over forty years earlier.

IN THOSE DAYS, THERE WAS ONLY THE OLD HOMESTEAD, RAMSHACKLE and barely livable after years of neglect. It had been his parents' home until they moved to Scottsdale when Ben was in high school. He hated Scottsdale and retreated to the ranch whenever he could. Then, when his parents died in a car accident his sophomore year at Stanford, he'd been shocked to learn they'd left the ranch to him. His younger siblings, Richard and Irene, had been sent to Chicago to live with their mother's sister, Aunt Ruby, and they had lost touch.

All through college, Ben Morgan had worked two and three jobs while pouring money into acquiring the land surrounding his parents' modest ranch. A senior in college, he now had hundreds of acres bought dirt cheap, waiting for him to come home.

As they drove up the driveway and parked next to the old farmhouse, he said, "Here we are," opening his arms and gesturing as they stepped out of his old Ford pickup.

"Oh," was all Leonora could manage as he reached out and took her hand.

His hand trembled in hers as he led her up to the house and opened the front door. "I know it's not much, but I have big plans."

Leonora smiled at her tall, lanky cowboy, squeezing his hand. "I'm sure you do, darlin'."

They walked through the musty rooms, cobwebs assailing them from every doorway.

The view from the back porch was spectacular, the pristine green valley stretching west to the mountains beyond. As they stood on the porch admiring it, she sighed. "You're right. It's beautiful."

"Not half as beautiful as you," he said as he bent down on one knee. "Marry me, Nora. If there's one thing I know, it's that I love you more than life itself. I can't imagine livin' a day without you at my side. If you hate the Valley, we'll sell and move. Wherever you want to go, as long as we're together." He pulled a small box from his jacket pocket and opened it to reveal a lovely emerald ring, the green stone surrounded by tiny diamonds.

She smiled down at him, gently caressing his cheek. "Ben Morgan, do you really think for one minute I'd ask you to leave your precious valley? It's all you've talked about since the day we met."

His face fell, and he gazed up, eyes filled with worry. "Does that mean you don't like it here?"

"Well, there's some fixing up and taming that's needed."

"I get it, honey. It's a lot to ask a city girl like you. We can talk about it and—"

"Pish tush! Of course I'll marry you! I've loved you since the day we met, and I can't wait to make a life here with you. I even spied a couple of nice spots on the way in where we could build a proper house. I mean, the view's lovely here, but I'm not sure the house is salvageable, and I—"

Ben jumped up and swooped her into his arms, twirling her around. "You said yes!"

"Course I did!"

"Then I'll build you a castle wherever you say. Ranch needs a name too. I have a good mind to call it Leonora!"

"Absolutely not. We'll think of something. Now, are you gonna put that ring on my finger and carry me over the threshold sometime today?"

Ben set her down and slipped the ring onto her tiny finger. It fit perfectly. "If you don't like it, we can exchange it."

"It's my birthstone, and it's perfect."

"I have to admit I did a little research about that. Now, are you sure about the threshold part? You know what that means."

Mischief in her gaze, she looked up at him. "I hope it means we're married and you can have your way with me."

"Oh, Nora, I love you!" he said, sweeping her up in his strong arms once more and carrying her into the bedroom.

LEONORA NUDGED HIM, BRINGING HIM BACK TO THE PRESENT. "WHAT time is it?"

He kissed her forehead as she turned to him. "Five thirty. We've got an hour. Wanna fool around?"

With a quick kiss, she hopped up, hands on hips. "Don't be ridiculous! It'll take me an hour to put on my face."

"It's a barbecue. 'Sides, your face looks beautiful."

"You always say that."

"'Cause it's true. Now come back here and snuggle."

"Tonight. *After* the barbecue."

He chuckled. "Something to live for."

Leonora limped, favoring her left hip as she moved about the room. He watched her for a few minutes before saying, "You okay, honey? Hip not too sore."

"I'm fine, and no mention of hips tonight! Remember, you promised. How'd things go with Harriet and her dad?"

"Fine. She's a trouper."

"I know Spark's worried about Helen. He told me the other night."

"Yes," Ben said, sitting up. "But she's strong like her daughter, and they'll both be surrounded by love."

His wife paused, her jeans in one hand, a blue-green top in the other. "Yes, they will. What a lot those two women went through all those years ago. Lucy, Clara, and Hazel too, poor dears."

He nodded. "You look really sexy in that robe. Come here, wife of mine."

Leonora waved her hand. "Not a chance! Now, up you go. Are you wearing those jeans and that shirt?"

"Thought I might."

She rolled her eyes. "Forty years and I still can't tame the cowboy in you. Now, come on, or we'll be late for dear Spark's extravaganza!"

Ben rose, gazing out the floor-to-ceiling windows that faced west over their backyard to the mountains beyond. They had almost as beautiful a view as the old homestead, which had been rebuilt and expanded and was now home to their eldest Ben, Maggie, and their kids. "Tents look great. Heaters all in place?" He referred to the enormous tent erected on their lawn, a second smaller one over the terrace, the site for tomorrow's wedding reception.

"All set, and thank goodness! It's meant to be chilly tomorrow. Someone in town even mentioned snow this morning."

"It's lucky getting married in the snow," he said as he rose and shed his clothes, heading for the shower.

"We're lucky, that's for sure," she said, opening her robe as she stepped closer. "Now you've gone and taken your clothes off. What's a girl to do?"

"What exactly," he murmured, slipping his hands under her robe as he guided her back to the bed.

"We don't have time for this," she whispered. "And what if the kids come in?"

As he nuzzled her neck, trailing kisses down to her breasts, he said, "We have time, and the kids're on their own. Spark'll hold down the fort. It's his party, thank goodness. 'Sides, no one cares about us old fogies."

"Old fogies, my eye," she whispered as her hand moved downward and began stroking and caressing.

As he took one luscious breast, then the other into his mouth, tweaking her nipples to attention, his fingers parted her legs and slipped into her warm, moist center. "Ready for me, darlin'?"

In answer, she opened her legs and guided him in, her body accepting him fully as they began to move in a familiar yet always surprising rhythm. Leonora arched her back and urged him deeper with every thrust, and Ben sighed, whispering her name over and over as they moved to climax.

After as they lay together, he kissed the tip of her nose. "Thank you, darlin'."

"You're welcome, cowboy. Confession? As much as I love my baby son and Harriet, I'd gladly stay here all night, just like this."

Ben grinned. "Me too, but let's go, kiddo." With a playful slap on her buttocks, he withdrew and stood up.

"I'll get you for that, Ben Morgan," she said, following him into the shower.

CHAPTER 10

"Where the hell are Mom and Dad?" Kyle asked his brother Sam as they waited at the entrance of Spark's barn, festooned with twinkle lights and greenery. The long tables were set with red-and-white-checkered tablecloths, and bouquets of flowers lined their centers. Harriet was nearby, talking with her sisters Hazel and Clara, and his brothers Ben and Robbie stood beside them.

"They'll be here," Sam said, patting his back.

Kyle shook his head. "Something's wrong, I can feel it. Mom's never late. We know this about her."

"Relax, buddy," Ben said. "Probably grabbed an afternoon delight and that set 'em back."

Kyle cringed. "I know they're still madly in love, but I could have done without that image, thanks. No one likes to think of their parents that way."

Robbie laughed, shaking his head. "Speaking of the happy couple, here they come."

"Thank God!" Kyle said as Spark greeted his longtime friends at the door.

Ben studied his brother. "Since when have you been so paranoid about Mom and Dad?"

Kyle leaned against his older brother and whispered, "Since I'm worried about Harriet and the arrival of her father and his horror show of a wife. I was hoping Mom, Dad, and Spark could act as buffers for Harriet and her mom."

"Well, you can relax, bro. Your bride's surrounded by her sisters, not to mention our two," he said as Beth, Ruthie, and Lucy joined the Winthrop sisters to the left of the barn door. "And here comes my lovely bride. No one messes with her."

"Hey, Mags," Kyle said as his beautiful sister-in-law approached them.

"Hi," she said, smiling as she hugged him. "You okay? For the man of the hour, you look a little green around the gills."

"Wedding jitters," her husband said, elbowing Kyle.

"Ha-ha," Kyle replied, eyes trained on the door as Jud and Rita Morgan stepped in and were greeted by Spark and his parents. He noticed that Helen had slipped from Spark's side and now stood among her daughters near the brothers. "Geez, what a shit show," he muttered, hurrying to Harriet's side.

"Come on," Ben said to Sam and Robbie. "Looks like little brother needs reinforcements."

"Well, I declare," Rita was saying as they neared the group. "I've never seen such a collection of drop-dead gorgeous men in my life! Must be something in the water. Hi, girls," she said, waving to Lucy, Clara, and Hazel. "Helen, good to see you. You're looking well."

Helen smiled. "Rita, Jud. How nice for Harriet and Kyle that you made the trip."

Rita leaned closer to her. "Not in Mr. Fancy Pants Foster's private jet, though. We flew economy, didn't we, Juddie?"

"That's enough, Rita." Jud's eyes flashed fire as he stepped forward to embrace his ex-wife. "Nice to see you, Helen."

Rita winked at Helen. "He's just jealous. Your Mr. Foster must be loaded with private jets, and look at this spread." She waved around the enormous finished barn, its beams as solid and steady as Spark himself.

"He's not my Mr. Foster. Just a dear friend."

"I wish I had friends like him."

Lucy nudged her sisters, and they stepped forward en masse except for Harriet, who seemed rooted to the floor, pale as a ghost. Lucy took hold of their father's arm. "Dad, Rita, why don't we find your seats and get you something from the bar. I believe your table is this way."

Helen moved to Harriet's side, slipping her arm around her daughter's shoulders. "How you doing, baby?"

"Fine, Mom. I'm fine. Even though inviting them was a huge mistake."

Kyle exchanged looks with Helen, then turned to his fiancée. "They're across the room, and that's the last we need to see them for the rest of the night, sweetheart. Come on, let's get a drink at the other bar."

"Sounds good to me," his brother Ben said, arm around Maggie.

Maggie patted his chest and said, "You go. I'd love a margarita. I'm just going to check on the kids."

"They're out back in Spark's fancy playground with Ruthie and Weezie. Boy, if those two aren't cut from the same cloth." Robbie pointed to the beautiful grassy play space with swings, a playhouse, slides, and jungle gyms that Spark had had built for his grandson Toby, son of his daughter Amy and Jeb Barnes.

Sam laughed. "Wolfie too. I saw him headed that way."

Will, Clara's husband, approached the group. "I see the old bastard got here in one piece."

Harriet gazed at her brother-in-law. "Yes."

"He's harmless," Will said, patting her shoulder. "Your sisters'll plant him somewhere, and you won't hear another peep out of him. Clara's appointed me as Rita's keeper tonight and tomorrow. God help me."

"Count me in," Robbie said.

Sam nodded. "Me too. Between us, we should be able to truss her up."

Harriet smiled. "Good luck with that. All of you. Now, husband-to-be, I believe I would like that drink."

CHAPTER 11

Leonora shook her head, gazing from Spark to her husband. "Well, we've met poor Harriet's father. Seems a bit of a broken shell to me, but her? What is she thinking with that hair?"

"My sentiments exactly," Spark said. "Never seen the likes of it."

"And you never will again if you're lucky!" she said. "Do you think Harriet and Helen are okay?"

Ben smiled, gazing across the barn. "I believe they're just fine. They're surrounded by women who love them *and* the Morgan posse."

"Bless them!" Leonora said. "And Spark, thank you for all this. As usual, you've outdone yourself. Everything looks beautiful. It'll be the fanciest barbecue I've ever attended. I can't wait to see what Aria's prepared."

"Gonna knock your socks off," Spark said. "Now let's round up Helen, grab a drink, and get this party started!"

Waitstaff passed all manner of hot hors d'oeuvres as Aria and her crew set up four buffet stations along the barn's perimeter. One featured ribs, chicken, and pulled pork, the second an assortment of salads and side dishes, the third a beautiful array of vegetarian offerings including grilled portabella mushrooms, savory nut-and-seed burgers, grilled sliced sweet potatoes, cauliflower shepherd's pie with Aria's homemade vegetable sausage, and roasted corn, peppers, and fennel. The fourth buffet was for the children and featured hot dogs, hamburgers, chicken, and four kinds of french fries—regular, curly, waffle, and sweet potato.

As Aria stood back surveying the vegetarian table, Jonas Miller found her, drink in hand. "So this is what you do."

Startled, she turned to face him. "Oh...hello." Despite the million-and-one things on her mind, she froze as she gazed into his blue-gray eyes. *Too bad he lives three thousand miles away.*

"Pretty impressive," he said, waving his hand toward the buffet.

"I hope so. Spark is a generous employer, and I want him to be pleased."

"Then he must be over the moon. This is incredible."

"I have a great staff. They come down from Portland for things like this. Thank God. I couldn't do it without them."

"Time for a drink?" he asked, unwilling to let her slip away.

"Hardly, but nice to see you. Sorry, I've got to get on with it."

He reached out and touched her arm. "You gonna be at the wedding tomorrow?"

"Yes, as a guest only. That is if I'm still standing."

"Save me a dance?"

Aria felt her face reddening, his touch electrifying as she wriggled out of it. "Of course... Excuse me."

Jonas watched her hurry off as his brother and Gail approached. "Romancing the chef?" Tim asked, giving him a look.

Jonas grinned. "Something like that."

The three strolled toward the nearest buffet and grabbed their plates.

"Great party, big brother," Richard Morgan said as he and Ben Senior stood watching their grandchildren in the backyard playground.

"Spark really knows how to throw a party. Always has."

"His chef is pretty amazing too."

"Yup. If I wasn't so stuffed, I'd go join the kids for roll and tumble."

"They're a gift, aren't they? Grandkids?" Richard said.

"The best."

"Who's that little blondie with your grandson?"

"That's Jasper. He's the son of our contractor Kevin Larrabee. Perry, his baby sister, is around somewhere. You know Kevin and Polly?"

"Sure do, and that's really nice of his wife Polly and her staff opening the Cottage tomorrow for the kids," Richard said.

"They'll have a ball. It'll be quite a crew, but Harley's daughter Willow's brought three of her college friends in to help out. They've got lots of activities planned. Give all their parents a chance to sightsee and the like."

"Lucky kids."

Ben nodded. "Sure are."

"Not to be a gossip," Richard said, "but what'd you think of Jud and Rita Winthrop?"

Ben gave his brother a look. "You want my honest opinion or the polite one?"

"Honest, of course."

"A red-hot mess. He looks about to keel over, and she seems to be a bit of a gold digger."

Richard laughed. "That's not far from Lucy's description, although she can be quite defensive about him. Apparently, the redhead left him a few years back to look for a 'Sugar Daddy' down in Palm Beach, then came crawling back when that plan failed."

"No wonder he looks about to keel over," Ben said, shaking his head. "We're sure lucky, aren't we, brother?"

"Don't I know it. Great wives, amazing kids, and all these new kids marrying into the family. Love 'em all."

"That's for damn sure."

"Great toast you made to Kyle and Harriet, by the way."

Ben's eyes softened. "Ruthie's the youngest, but Kyle's our baby too. Almost lost him and Nora when he was born, then again last year on the trail. Miss him now, but I'm glad he's with family back east."

"Everyone in the village loves him, and they're so grateful he's there. He's a wonderful vet."

Ben nodded, gazing across the crowd and spying his wife approaching. She was clearly favoring her leg but trying hard not to show it. "Here comes Nora. Probably got some marching orders for me."

"Here you are," she said. "Havin' fun?" she asked, turning to her brother-in-law.

"Sure am."

"I'm glad to see that sanity prevailed and you two are not mixed up in that melee!" she said, watching the children run back and forth. "Our daughter will never grow up, I'm afraid."

At that moment, Ruthie jumped out of the playhouse where she'd been hiding and roared. Wolfie and Weezie Morgan followed, each scooping up children as they circled the grass.

Richard laughed. "Mine either. And look at my vineyard manager!"

Leonora turned to her husband. "What do you think, Bennie? I'm getting tired, and there's so much to do in the morning."

"I'm ready when you are darlin'."

"Lucy and I are right behind you," Richard said, scanning the room to where he spied his wife and her sister Hazel hustling their father and Rita out. "Soon as she dispatches her dad."

Leonora rolled her eyes. "Such a problem. Poor Harriet. Now, what are your plans for tomorrow?"

"Lucy and I thought we might take a trail ride. Some of the others are organizing it. Early in the morning."

"Very ambitious. I know Spark's fleet and my Cowbelles will be out for guests who want tours, but of course you all know the place well."

Richard's eyes shone with warmth as he hugged his sister-in-law. "This is all incredible. Leonora. Thank you so much."

"Oh, pish tush! We love every minute. Now, get a good night's sleep. We'll be dancing into the wee hours tomorrow!"

"Happy, darlin'?" Ben asked as he and Leonora headed for the Range Rover.

"Happy I'm about to get off my feet."

"You okay?"

"More than okay. It went well, didn't it? I'm so proud of Kyle and Harriet. Your toast was perfect and your oldest son's too, even if a bit inappropriate. Honestly. I could throttle him sometimes."

"Now he's *my* oldest?"

"You know what I mean. I love Ben, but he's as fresh as can be. I'm so grateful that he has Maggie to keep him in line most of the time."

"Love you, darlin'," he said, opening her door and helping her into the Rover.

"Love you too." She drew him down for a kiss, then added, "Now get this car started and get me home."

CHAPTER 12

Spark's fleet of cars was kept busy Saturday taking guests for tours of the ranch and valley as well as shuttling people to activities. Every horse in the Morgan's Run stables was saddled and ready for early morning trail rides. Maggie and Emma had ridden from their house to the barn and were ready to guide their guests. Emma rode her pony, Sunny, and Maggie, her huge draft horse, Tabasco. One of the ranch's first mustang rescues, Tabasco's size had frightened any potential border patrol agent the moment they clapped eyes on him. Finally, Ben Senior made the decision that Maggie should have him, as horse and woman had bonded during the yearlong training.

Lucy and Richard and her kids, Amy and Rob, joined Kyle and his father and brothers in "Emma's party." Maggie took a group that included the Miller siblings as well as Rich, Ben, Wolfie, Weezie, and Pam Morgan, along with Pam's fiancé, Sandy Rodriguez.

"That woman sure knows how to fill out a pair of jeans," Cousin Ben said to Sandy as the group followed Maggie up the trail.

"I heard that!" Weezie said. "What are we, chopped liver, brother dear?"

"Absolutely not, but we see you every day. Now, Maggie Morgan, on the other hand..."

"Is a married woman," Pam said, swatting him on the arm as the horses passed each other.

"And a woman who has excellent hearing," Maggie called from the front of the line. "Be careful up here and take it slow. Lots of loose pebbles and sand."

"The place is amazing, isn't it?" Jonas Miller said as they reached a rise and began following the ridge. He rode alongside his sisters, Rachel and Karen, and his older brother Rex Junior. Their brother Brick and his wife and kids had taken a picnic out to Valley Stables with Clara and Will's family.

"Sure is," Karen said, gazing back to Rich Morgan, who followed her and did not look particularly comfortable on Tara, one of the gentler stable horses. "Doing okay back there?" she asked.

"Oh, just fine," he called. "Not the rider most of you are, I'm afraid."

"I hear you, buddy," Jonas said. "The rest of my family lived on horses growing up, but I preferred the reliable kind that ran on gasoline."

Karen laughed. "Yeah, right. Reliable? You put more of Mom and Dad's vehicles out of commission with your engineering prowess than I can count."

"Where are your mom and dad this morning?" Weezie asked. "I'd have thought they'd love this."

"They went out yesterday with Gail and Tim," Karen said. "Mom's gathered the Yarners for a 'support Helen' excursion. I think they're eating in town to escape the ex and Rita, who commandeered one of Spark's SUVs this morning for the 'deluxe tour,' as Rita called it. She announced at breakfast that they'd be 'taking lunch on the terrace,' so the rest of us have made plans to be anywhere but there."

"What about your dad?"

"With Spark," Karen said. "They were going out to the thoroughbred farm, then probably eating at Spark's. Anyone's invited there. Aria's gonna put out food around noon."

"Good to know," Jonas said.

For the next fifteen minutes, they made their slow descent down to the valley. Maggie waited below as riders inched downward, a wide open meadow in front of her stretching a mile or so to the river.

"Come on down!" she called, waving her hand. When all horses and riders had reached level ground, she asked," How's everyone doing?"

"Great!" Weezie said. "I'm in love with Raffles."

Maggie smiled. "That's good, 'cause he can be skittish with a less experienced rider. He's one of our rescues. Not a wild horse, but he and his brother Thor were found starving to death on an old farm. They almost didn't make it. Nick Parker brought them back to life."

"He's amazing with horses, isn't he?" Weezie said dreamily.

"Yes, we're lucky to have him. And you're lucky to have Gus. He's an extraordinary trainer. Now, folks, what do you think? We can keep along at this pace or let the horses go and have a gallop to the river. They love it."

Everyone cheered except Rich. "You guys go ahead. Tara and I will go at our own pace."

Maggie smiled. "You can try, but she's gonna want to follow Raine and the others. You and I could stay back and I'll take her lead. Weezie can lead everyone to the river."

"Oh, what the heck," Rich said. "I don't wanna spoil the fun. If I fall off and break my neck, someone better come back for me."

"You sure?" Maggie eyed him. "We're all about safety here."

"I'll be fine," he said. "Off you go."

Maggie nudged her huge mount, and Tabasco took off, the others at their side. True to form, Tara stayed right behind Raine as the horses raced across the open meadow. Rich held on for dear life and managed to stay in the saddle until they slowed at the river's edge. Maggie slipped off Tabasco and led him to the water, and the others followed suit. "Who wants a snack?" she asked as riders pulled water bottles and drinks from their packs. She passed out trail mix and power bars, always watching the horses out of the corner of her eye. "We'll ride along the river till the path joins the Loop Trail, then it's only a short ride back. We may meet Emma's group. They rode the

Loop, and I think the trail that ends at the Dillons', so they should be heading back now too."

Sure enough, twenty minutes later as they left the river and ascended to the Loop Trail ringing Morgan's Run, they spied riders heading up from the south. "Hey, Mommy," Emma called as they drew near.

"Hi, princess! Did you lead everyone the whole way?"

"She sure did," Ben, her father, called from right behind her.

"Why don't you all go ahead of us, then," Maggie said.

"Okay, Mommy. Ready guys?" Emma called, looking behind her.

As the other group passed by, Ben Senior waved. "That's my granddaughter. Ain't she something?"

"You guys are so damn lucky," Jonas said, watching the others ride past. "To be able to do this every day."

"We have horses at home, brother dear," Karen said.

"Yeah, but not this," he said, opening his arms.

"Our family dreamer," Karen said, smiling at Rich beside her.

"Nothing wrong with that," Jonas said, waving as Lucy's teenagers rode past, followed by Sam and Robbie Morgan. "Lucky thing none of our parents got the memo about population control and having smaller families."

"Ha-ha!" Karen said, rolling her eyes as their group headed up and onto the Loop.

CHAPTER 13

When most of the morning riding party arrived at Spark's, they found lunch laid out along the wide kitchen counter. Rex Miller Senior and Spark were in the sunroom chatting, and others were scattered in the kitchen and dining room. Jonas grabbed a plate of food and headed to the sunroom.

"Hey, guys," he said, taking a seat on a wide comfortable patio sofa opposite the older men.

"Hey, yourself, son. How was the ride?"

"Great. Thanks for all this." He held up his plate, which included a sandwich, some leftover ribs, and salad.

"Thank Aria and her gang. They whipped everything up for us."

"Where is she anyway?" Jonas asked, hoping his inquiry sounded casual.

"Took her crew into town for lunch before they fly out. I expect they're headed to Grenville about now. Plane's waitin' on them whenever they arrive."

Disappointed, Jonas took a bit of a delicious roast beef baguette. "Your valley's beautiful, Spark."

"Sure is. Minute I laid eyes on it, I knew I'd live here someday. What about you, son? Do you live in Horseshoe Crab Cove?"

"Sort of. I keep an apartment there, but I travel almost constantly."

"Your dad's been tellin' me. Sounds like you do real interestin' work."

"It's a solid company, and they've been good to me."

"Well, if you ever want a change, we're always looking for good engineers. My companies are based in Portland, but we go all over the world. I'm working with my team to develop a plant outside of Tucson. Should be up and runnin' by next year. We'll be hirin' for that site soon. Havin' them close by means that even in retirement, I can sick my nose in. Think about it, son. I don't want to poach you from your present company. That's one of my rules. Whoever comes to work for me, it's his or her decision."

Jonas looked at his father, who nodded. "True story. I didn't say a thing."

"I'm honored, Spark. Thank you. Of course I'll think about it. I'd be crazy not to. Your companies are doing the kind of work that I admire and want to be a part of someday."

Spark winked at Rex Miller before turning to his son. "Just say the word, and I'll put you in touch with my personnel director."

They talked awhile longer before they were joined by Helen, Frankie, Jonas's mother, and his aunt Grace. "The Yarners have returned," Jonas said, rising to allow the women to sit.

"Don't hurry off on our account," Faith Miller said, patting her son's shoulder.

"How was lunch?" Spark asked.

"By the looks of things, not nearly as sumptuous as yours," Faith said. "But lots of fun. What a great town, and your stables are very impressive."

Spark beamed. "We're tryin'. Where'd you gals eat anyway?"

"The Bulldog," Helen said.

"That ole saloon?" Spark said.

"It was great," Frankie said. "Best burger I've ever had."

Spark nodded. "Made with the best Valley beef from the ranch or the Dillons'."

Helen smiled. "Can't believe you've never taken me there before."

"Well, I wasn't sure it was fittin' for an East Coast lady like yerself."

Jonas observed his mother and her friends, who always seemed to morph into teenagers when they got together. "What is this place? Some kind of dive bar?"

Frankie grinned. "A saloon. Not a dive. Owner's terrific too. Couldn't have been more solicitous to us old bags."

"Wonderful old photographs too," Helen said. "I recognized Maggie's dad, Ned."

"The finest wrangler the Valley's ever produced," Spark said. "Or at least that's the legend."

"Well, I'll have to stop in before I head home," Jonas said.

"Good luck squeezing it in," Faith said, coming to sit on the arm of her husband's chair. "What do you think, honey? Should we head back to the Lodge? Won't be long before the wedding."

Rex stood, offering her his hand. "I'm ready when you are. Whaddya say, gang? Let's round up your sisters and commandeer one of the SUVs."

"I'll get one of the drivers," Spark said, rising. "Don't want to be late for the big event!"

CHAPTER 14

In Nora's dreams, Ben's strong arms held her as he stepped over the dusty bedroom threshold. The old bed was covered with a faded patchwork quilt, nubbly but soft as he set her down gently. "Darlin', you are the most beautiful thing I've ever seen."

"You too," she whispered, tiny fingers caressing his jaw. "Now I think I deserve a little kiss, cowboy, don't you?"

"More than a little one," he said, capturing her lips, his tongue opening her mouth and tasting her sweetness. He left no doubt that he wanted more, much more as the kiss went deeper and his hands moved to caress her full, soft breasts. As he slowly unbuttoned her blouse, she gasped. His lips moved down between her breasts, then he parted her lacy pink bra, taking one breast, then the other into his mouth.

Leonora sighed, arching up to him, giving herself to this man she loved beyond all reason.

Ben drew back, staring down at her and smiling, his blue eyes full of love. "You sure about this, Nora?"

"Never more sure of anything," she said as she unzipped her slacks and slipped them off revealing pink lacy panties.

He whistled. "Wow, almost too pretty to touch."

"But you will touch them as you quickly take them off me!"

"In that case, I'd better get rid of some of my duds." He slipped out of his jeans, his erection straining the front of his boxers. As he gazed down at her, he sensed a change. "What's the matter, sweetie?"

"I've... I've... Well, the truth is that despite my sassy talk, I've never seen a man. I've never been with a man."

"We can stop right now, sweetie. I only want what makes you comfortable."

She reached up, her arms circling his neck, eyes soft. "You make me feel comfortable, Ben Morgan, and I know that however you plan to get that inside of me, it will be right,"

"Oh so right," he said, fingers gently slipping her panties down as he parted her legs. "I'll only go as far as you want, baby. You say stop if you're not comfortable, okay?"

Teeth biting her lower lip, she nodded. Eyes wide open, she gasped as he moved between her legs, probing as he found her warm wetness. He found her clit and began a slow, loving caress that soon had her panting for him. "You ready for me?" he said, his voice husky.

"It's your call. You say the word."

In answer, Leonora arched against him. "Now...now...now...before I go insane!"

He slipped a condom from his jeans pocket, opened it, and sheathed himself. Kissing her deeply, he moved between her legs. "We'll take it nice and slow, my love."

She nodded as he made a tentative thrust, all the while gazing down, making sure he wasn't hurting her. Leonora's eyes never left his as he went deeper and deeper until she wondered if he might cleave her in half. As he reached her deepest center, something happened to Leonora. For the first time in her life she felt complete and whole. She felt loved and nurtured beyond her wildest dreams. "I love you so!" she cried as she arched again, begging him to go deeper.

"Not as much as I love you," he whispered as they moved in tandem to a startling, breathless climax.

In the aftermath, he nuzzled her neck, kissing and whispering words of love. "Thank you, darlin'."

"You're welcome, cowboy," Leonora said as she kissed the long scar along his shoulder, a riding accident from his youth.

"Penny for your thoughts," Ben said, startling her back to the present.

Leonora's eyes flew open. "Oh! I must've dozed off." She reached up to stroke his cheek. "And my thoughts were X-rated."

"The best kind. Tell me."

"I was thinking about our first time. In the farmhouse."

"That was somethin', wasn't it? Don't think we got much sleep that night, did we?"

She smiled at him. "And boy, was I sore the next day, but it was worth it."

"Sure was. Want to give it a go now?"

"No farmhouse. No patchwork quilt, and the wedding's in an hour. But you can help me get cleaned up in our big ole shower."

"You are a wicked woman! That's my best kind of cleanup."

Suffused with warmth after making love in the shower, they emerged from the bathroom, Leonora in a thick white terry robe, Ben with a towel wrapped around his waist.

Her fingers caressed his strong, still-muscular chest. "You really know how to steam up a room, husband of mine. Can't do my makeup in there."

He patted her bottom, pulling her closer.

Leonora felt him grow hard against her. "Oh no you don't! No time! You're insatiable, Mr. Morgan." She gave him a quick kiss on the cheek then stepped back.

"You're to blame there, honey." He headed for his dressing room, calling over his shoulder, "You know we should go on a honeymoon after the new year. Whaddya think? After all this, we deserve it."

"Have you forgotten? This cripple needs a hip replacement."

"Well then, as soon as you're back on your feet. Anywhere you want to go!"

"Anywhere?"
He poked his head around the closet door. "Anywhere."
"Hmm... That's something to motivate me in recovery."
"Good!"

CHAPTER 15

Clusters of bright blooms filled the tiny chapel. The congregation settled in, and the music began. After the parents had taken their seats, a throng of little children entered. The girls held baskets of rose petals and wore white dresses with pale blue satin sashes, the boys were in charcoal suits that matched Kyle's groomsmen. Groomsmen and boys wore blue ties the same color as the little girls' sashes and Harriet's bridesmaids' dresses.

The wedding party children included Emma and her little brother, Lynn and Gus Casey's two older children Dulcie and Cal, and Toby Barnes. Charlotte Langdon and Lily Dillon also toddled down the aisle hand in hand, and Jasper Larrabee, son of Kevin and Polly, marched alongside the tiny girls far away from his partner in crime, Ben the third.

"Oh aren't they all precious!" Leonora said, leaning her head against her husband's shoulder.

Then came the beautiful bridesmaids, Harriet's three sisters, her maid of honor, Karen Miller, Maggie, Beth Dillon and Ruthie Morgan Langdon. The groomsmen waited, lined up beside Kyle. They included Kyle's three brothers, Harley, and Kyle's college roommate, John.

As the bridesmaids lined up, Karen leaned toward Maggie and whispered, "Oh my God! How do you get anything done around here? I'd spend my whole day gawking at handsome cowboys if I lived here."

Maggie smiled. "You get used to it."

At that moment, the chapel doors reopened and Harriet stepped in on the arm of her father. She had originally planned to walk down the aisle alone, but changed her mind the previous evening. Jud had asked with a sad yearning in his cloudy blue eyes, and Harriet had swallowed hard and answered, "Okay, Dad, if you want."

EVEN WITH THE THREAT OF SNOW, THE NIGHT HAD WARMED AND THE heaters were off, the tent awash with color and warmth. Candles lined the long tables, which were decorated with a blend of east and west. Seashells, cactus, and silver figurines shimmered in the candlelight. Flowers were everywhere along the beams of the tent, in urns along the walls and at the tent doors. A sit-down dinner, the tables were set with colorful linens, local pottery, and gleaming silver flatware. Staff from the Lodge and a number of local people had been brought in as waitstaff and bartenders, with Carmela and Raoul overseeing every detail. Leonora and Ben had begged them to come as guests and had offered to hire caterers, but they refused. The Dillons' chef, Jon Wilson, was also on hand to assist, as was their housekeeper, Neecy.

"What a lovely ceremony that was," Helen said as she and Spark stood next to Leonora and Ben at the end of the rapidly dwindling receiving line.

"Yes, and what a lovely couple too. We're blessed as you are. That was very kind of your dear Harriet to allow Jud to walk her down."

Helen nodded. "Yes."

"Strong, brave girl," Leonora said, reaching over to squeeze Helen's hand.

At Kyle and Harriet's request, the meal, from appetizers to dessert, was all Southwest cuisine and included all the couple's favorites. During the cocktail hour, waiters passed many varieties of quesadillas, tiny wedge salads on skewers, enchilada roll-ups, shrimp avocado crostini, vegetarian and meat-filled taquitos, along with bowls of guacamole, salsa, and chips. Dinner began with cool savory gazpacho, then waiters served fish, meat or vegetarian entrées with all manner of roasted vegetables. The salad course was a festive chopped salad served with a cilantro lime dressing. Finally, dessert was a creamy flan topped with fresh berries in lieu of wedding cake.

Richard Morgan clapped his older brother on the back. "I love our Callie back home, but I'd be happy to steal Carmela and Raoul from you."

Ben Senior grinned, waving a forkful of beef tenderloin. "Not a chance."

Leonora winked at Lucy. "Forget your stomachs, you two. Just look around. So many beautiful couples everywhere."

Spark nodded. "There's a lotta love under this tent."

"You're right about that," Helen said, reaching over to touch Spark's hand. It was an intimate gesture and Ben and Leonora exchanged looks. Spark and Helen were steadfast in maintaining their friendship status, but this looked like something more.

"There go the bride and groom," Ben said as Kyle led Harriet to the dance floor. Strains of Lonestar's "Amazed" began, and Kyle drew her into his arms, kissing her forehead as they began moving to the music.

"So happy," Leonora said, tears in her eyes as she watched the couple.

Ben put his arm around her. "Me too, baby."

Soon other dancers took to the floor, including Maggie and Ben Morgan, the pair that locals called the "the beautiful couple." She wore a satiny blue sheath that hugged every luscious curve. Ben's attention never left his wife, love shining in his chestnut eyes.

Jonas Miller led Aria onto the floor, and Spark whistled under his breath. "Now there's a surprise. Guess I'm gonna have to insist he come work for me or I could lose my chef!"

"Are you serious?" Leonora asked.

"Dead serious. About the job, at least. We'd love to have him. If he stays back east and takes her with him, I'll be taking all my meals with you two."

CHAPTER 16

Jonas drew Spark's raven-haired chef into his arms. "Glad you made it back from the airport in time," he said. "You look amazing, by the way." Aria wore a sleeveless dress of gray and navy floral jacquard inset with off-centered white twill panels. The plunging neckline flattered her gorgeous breasts, and the dress's flouncy skirt, two inches above her knees, showcased her lovely long legs. Four-inch gray stiletto heels and simple silver jewelry complemented the outfit perfectly.

"Thanks. You look pretty amazing yourself."

"But I'm not wearing that dress."

"It cost me three weeks' salary, but no matter. I'm happy with it."

"Me too." He pulled her closer until her soft breasts pressed against his chest. Instantly, he felt himself grow hard. *Whoa boy, watch yourself.*

She felt his erection and smiled up at him. "You doin' okay?"

"I'd be a lot better if we were off this dance floor and out of this tent."

"Oh?"

The song ended, and he took her hand. "What do you say to a walk?"

Aria smiled. "I say yes."

As they strolled out, Tim Miller nudged Gail. "Looks like my brother's found a friend."

"I'm glad," she said, nuzzling against her husband.

It didn't take long for Jonas and Aria to find a secluded spot behind the Big House barn. Several benches lined the back wall of the barn that afforded lovely views of the valley and mountains to the west. They ignored them and the view as Jonas led her to the wall and pulled her into his arms. "I've wanted to do this since the first time I laid eyes on you."

"Me too," she said, then his lips captured hers in a deep kiss, their tongues entwined, their desire mutual.

As his hands trailed down to cup her breasts, Aria sighed and gave herself to the sensations coursing through her body. He drew the neck of her dress apart and took one breast, then the other into his mouth. It was all she could do not to scream as a glorious orgasm overtook her.

"You okay?" he whispered huskily as his hands moved south.

"More than okay," she said, trailing kisses along his neck.

"Is this okay?" He slid her panties down, then his fingers moved up her thighs.

She nodded, afraid to speak, overwhelmed with desire and slightly frightened by the size of him. As his fingers worked their magic, she slowly unzipped his slacks and released him, gasping as she took him in her hands.

"I'm gonna explode soon," he said.

"Not unless you're inside me."

"I'm sorry, sweetie. I don't have protection."

"I'm on the pill," she whispered. "It's a long story. I'll tell you later I'm clean, promise."

"Me too." Grasping her thighs, he lifted her, wrapping her legs around him as he backed her against the barn wall. The tip of him stroked her moist warmth. Aria gasped, throwing her head back as his tongue traced the contours of her long, slender neck.

"I'll go slow," he whispered, moving deeper.

Aria grasped his strong shoulders, her fingers digging into him. The feel of him thrusting deep inside her was both painful and the most intense pleasure she had ever experienced. She arched her back, begging him to go deeper. Finally, she reached a heart-stopping orgasm, clapping her hand over her mouth to muffle her screams. His release came soon after as their bodies moved together in delicious tandem.

When Jonas looked down, he was surprised to find her lovely cheeks streaked with tears. "Hey, are you okay?" he whispered.

She nodded. "I did it. At thirty-one, I'm a virgin no more."

Incredulous, he stared down at her face bathed in moonlight. "What?"

"Thank you for making my first time so spectacular," she said, stroking his face.

Gently, he withdrew from her and set her down. Then, cradling her in his arms, he carried her to one of the benches. "I can't believe it. Are you kidding me?"

She shook her head. "I know, I know... I come across as a vixen, woman of the world, whatever, but I've never actually 'done it' until now. When I was younger, I was just scared. The past few years, I was scared the right guy might never came along."

"Why me?"

"'Cause I'm tired of watching all the people around here crazy in love and clearly having wild, unbridled sex all over the place."

"Is that a ranch expression—unbridled sex?"

"Ha-ha."

"So I'm your guinea pig?" he said.

"It's not like that. I'm... I was very attracted to you. And then tonight is so romantic. It seemed like the perfect moment."

He turned and kissed her. "Thank you for giving me such an incredible gift. It was perfect."

Her fingers caressed his cheek. "I should be thanking you. Even though I was terrified when I...when I felt you...how big. I didn't think we'd fit, but we did."

Jonas grinned. "The miracle of foreplay. It opens many doors. Much as I'd like to open the door many more times tonight, we'd better get back. I'm supposed to be giving a toast."

Aria found her panties, and he pulled himself together. "How do I look?" she said.

"Perfect."

"I mean am I a wreck?"

"I hope you look like you've been well fucked," he said, hands gently smoothing her long, wavy hair.

"I hope not!" She giggled as he took her hand and led her back to the tent.

At the entrance to the tent, Jonas kissed her palm. "Gotta find my brothers. I'll hook up with you later, okay?"

Aria nodded, wandering dreamlike through the crowd. Harriet caught up with her near the bar. "Having a good time?" she asked, smiling at the woman who had become her dearest friend in the Valley.

Aria grinned. "I just found out what everyone else in this tent has known for years. Sex is the most incredible experience in the world."

"You didn't."

"We did, and it was beyond spectacular. I mean, I know it can't last, but even one night is something to cherish."

"Why can't it last?"

"Look at him, then look at me. Besides geography, he's incredibly handsome, successful, and intelligent, and then there's me."

"As Leonora would say, pish tush to that kind of thinking. Uh-oh, it appears they're gearing up for the toasts. I'd better find Kyle. I'm so happy for you!"

As she watched Harriet hurry toward her husband, Aria felt at peace and happier than she'd ever been.

CHAPTER 17

Leonora sighed. "I love sitting under a tent the day after a wedding."

She was having breakfast with Ben, Spark, Helen, Rose, and Sam, Hazel Winthrop, and her college roommate, Suzie Miller Harding. Harriet and Kyle had booked a room at the Red Mesa Inn for a one-night honeymoon, but they were due back in the early afternoon in time for the evening's anniversary party.

Heaters blazed all around them to ward off the early morning chill. Carmela had set out bowls of fruit, baskets of muffins, and warmers of eggs, bacon, and sausage. Juices and coffee urns sat at the end of the table. After enjoying Aria's breakfast buffet, Spark and Helen had popped over to say hello and see if they needed anything. They were now sipping coffee and tea as they chatted with their dear friends. Suzie had been close friends with Spark's wife, Patsy, and later Leonora. In fact, it was Suzie who had brought Ben and Leonora together.

Suzie leaned back, taking a sip of coffee. "I sure love it here. It's amazing to think how far we've come."

Leonora patted her hand. "We were quite a bunch, weren't we?"

Suzie winked at Ben. "I can still remember the day you met your handsome cowboy."

Ben smiled, raising his mug in a toast. "And you sure saved my bacon that weekend in Los Angeles."

"You mean the worse two days of my life," Leonora said. "If it hadn't been for you, Spark, and Patsy, I might have committed murder." They referred to the weekend trip the friends had taken to Bel Air so Ben could meet Leonora's parents.

BEN'S FIRST GLIMPSE OF THE POSH RESIDENTIAL COMMUNITY IN THE foothills of the Santa Monica Mountains had been the entrance gates off Sunset Boulevard. He whistled as they made their way through the gates to streets lined with towering trees, sweeping lawns and enormous mansions. "Wow," he had exclaimed. "Looks like we're in a Hollywood movie."

Seated in the front seat of Leonora's little roadster, Suzie had turned back and said, "You are, and you haven't even seen the house yet. Keep an eye out for the stars. They're thick as thieves around here."

All turrets, chimneys, and towers, Leonora's home was in the same neo-Gothic style as the exclusive Bel Air Country Club where Thomas Brooks and his wife, Lily had insisted upon taking them to dinner shortly after their arrival.

"What'd I tell you?" Suzie said as they drove up the circular drive. They were met at the door by a tall dark-haired man dressed in a black morning coat.

"This is Seamus," Leonora said. "He's our house manager. He's in charge of everything, thank goodness! Hi, Seamus." The daughter of the house hopped out and hugged the man, whose ramrod straight posture folded as he returned her embrace.

"Hello, miss. Good to have you home."

Introductions followed. Seamus assisted with the luggage, aided by a younger man, Oliver, whom Leonora introduced as the gardener. The party headed in through the ornate entry hall with its twenty-foot windows and enormous chandelier, up a grand staircase to their rooms. As they ascended, Seamus explained that her parents were out but would meet them at the country club promptly at seven.

"Typical," Leonora said.

Ben saw the disappointment in her eyes. For all its grandness, her childhood home seemed cold and lifeless, a sad lonely place for a child. "What's the dress code tonight?" he had asked. "I've got some nice slacks, but didn't think to bring a jacket and tie."

"Me either," Spark had said, clearly amused by the situation.

Seamus studied the two men for several minutes before saying, "I'll fetch two ties from Mr. Brooks' collection. He won't mind, but he's considerably shorter than you gentlemen, so you'll have to borrow two of the Club's emergency jackets. They have them in all sizes."

"Works for me," Ben said as he was ushered into his room. Except for Patsy and Spark, who were married by then, they each had their own room with an adjacent marble bathroom.

Leonora's room was just down the hall from her fiancé's. As Seamus departed to fetch the ties, she whispered, "I'll find you tonight. Don't worry."

When they arrived at the club, the maître d' informed Leonora that her parents were waiting in the bar. After obtaining sports jackets for the men, the four headed to the main bar. Ben's first impression of Leonora's parents was not a positive one. Socialite Lily Brooks was short and petite, her blonde shoulder-length hair perfectly coiffed in what appeared to be an imitation Marilyn Monroe style. She wore a shimmering silver cocktail dress and enough diamonds to buy a small country. She bore a remarkable physical resemblance to her daughter, but that was where the similarity ended. Her husband was her height, slightly portly, his salt-and-pepper hair slicked back with thick pomade. He appeared to be at least a decade older than his wife, but it was difficult to tell. He wore a dark suit and a red cravat tied jauntily round his neck.

"Well, here you are, then," Lily said, leaning forward to plant air kisses on both her daughter's cheeks.

"Hello, Mother, Dad. You remember Patsy and Suzie, but I don't think you've met Patsy's husband, Spark Foster?"

Spark extended his hand, which Nora's father took and his wife ignored.

"And this is Ben," Leonora went on. "My fiancé."

Thomas Brooks shook his hand as Lily Brooks nodded, her hands firmly at her sides. Her expression resembled that of someone who had just bitten into a lemon. "Well, well... This is a surprise."

"Evenin'," Ben said, bowing slightly. "It's a pleasure to finally meet you both. Leonora has told me so much about you."

"Well, isn't that nice," Lily said. "We've heard absolutely nothing about you, Mr. Morgan."

"Ben, please."

"Shall we go into dinner?" Thomas said.

Dinner conversation had been strained and stilted, Leonora on the edge of her seat all evening. A master of jocularity, Spark kept up a lively repartee with Suzie, which saved the evening from complete disaster. Occasionally, one of the Brookses chimed in to interrogate Ben, but mostly they stayed silent, their attention frequently diverted by passersby to whom they waved and occasionally rose to say hello.

As they said good night in their home's cavernous entryway, Lily Brooks said, "I've arranged a tour of the Japanese Garden for tomorrow morning, then you're on your own until dinner, which will be here. We've invited a few friends."

Her daughter's face fell, but she stood silent. When the parents left them, the group headed upstairs, giggles and laughter in their wake.

When they were all in Spark and Patsy's room, Leonora said, "I'm so sorry, gang. I'd hoped it would be our weekend, not one of Mother's civic projects."

Patsy hugged her. "Not to worry, dearie. We'll make it fun and be back at school in no time."

That night, Leonora had come to him, and they made love quietly in his grand queen-size bed. "I'd love to stay till morning," she whispered shortly after midnight, "but I dare not provoke the dragon lady."

Ben kissed her softly. "I love you, Nora. Soon enough, we'll be together every night."

Leonora stroked his strong jaw. "I love you too. Now you see why I was dreading this? Let's just get through it and ignore whatever they say."

THE TRIP TO THE HANNAH CARTER JAPANESE GARDEN SEVERAL BLOCKS from the Brookses' mansion was ever after referred to as the "LA Inquisition." From the moment they set foot in the lush, beautiful setting inspired by the gardens of Kyoto, Lily Brooks interrogated Ben about his future plans. They had little freedom to admire the gardens or structures—a main gate, garden house, bridges, and shrine—that were built in Japan and reassembled in Bel Air. As Ben and the others admired the antique stone carvings, water basins, and lanterns as well as the five-tiered pagoda and symbolic rocks from Japan, Lily badgered him about the size of his ranch and what he planned to do with it.

Leonora finally managed to break away from her mother and announced that they wanted to eat at her favorite diner in Los Angeles. "Well, I'll skip that, darling. Have a lovely afternoon, and I'll see you later for cocktails."

The four friends spent a carefree afternoon exploring the more bohemian areas of the city. As they reluctantly headed home, Ben said, "Hey, sweetheart, I almost forgot. Should Spark and I purchase some duds for dinner? Are your parents all right with casual?"

"No, but I don't care. Patsy, Suzie, and I will wear slacks, so we'll present a united front!"

At his own dinner table, Thomas Brooks seemed to come to life, relating many stories about his life as one of the most sought-after Hollywood agents. His client list included some of the top stars of the day, and his anecdotes, while discreet, revealed much about the behind-the-scenes life in the city.

Later, Leonora snuggled in Ben's bed again, running her fingers across his strong chest. "I can't wait to get back to the apartment," she whispered.

Ben kissed the top of her head. "Me too. We should probably get an early start."

"My parents want to take us to breakfast. Just you and me. Do you mind awfully?"

"Of course not." He drew her closer.

"I love you, Ben Morgan. Please remember that, whatever happens tomorrow morning."

"Right back atcha, darlin'."

They went to a small breakfast café just outside the gates of Bel Air. As they sat enjoying quiches and sipping coffee, Thomas said, "So tell us more about your ranch, son."

"It's about a hundred acres now, but I'm saving and expanding it as I can," Ben said. "I bought out my siblings last year, so it's all mine."

"And the bank's, I imagine," the older man said.

"Not for too long, sir."

Lily set down her fork. "Do you honestly see our sophisticated, well-educated daughter living on a farm?"

Her face a mask of fury, Leonora said, "This is my choice."

"No, my darling," her mother said. "It's ours, and we forbid it. We made discreet inquiries about the property and had an agent visit the Valley a few weeks ago."

"What?" Leonora shouted, her green eyes ablaze.

"Now calm down, sweetie. It was for your protection. He came back with lots of photos and financial projections. It's just not viable. We will not allow you to throw your life away in the middle of the desert. There will be no money, no wedding, no nothing."

Ben cleared his throat. "With all due respect, Mrs. Brooks, I'm not sure what your spy uncovered, but the land and its prospects have been carefully researched. I have a business plan and—"

"Enough!" Thomas said. "My wife has spoken. We will not sanction this marriage, and that's that."

Leonora stood, upsetting her glass, sending orange juice splashing to the floor. "Let's go Ben. We'll take a cab to the house, collect our things, and be gone."

"Now hold on, young lady."

"No, Daddy, I won't. I wish you only the best, and you will receive an invitation to the wedding. It's going to be in Stanford, by the way. Goodbye." With those words, she grabbed Ben's hand and they exited the café. He waved over his shoulder at her parents, whom neither ever saw again.

"Hey, buddy, you're a million miles away," Spark said, placing a hand on his friend's shoulder.

Ben smiled. "Old ghosts."

"Better to leave 'em. This is gonna be some shindig tonight."

"Sure is."

Sam observed the two. Finally, he said, "Rose and I are going over to see her folks this morning, then heading into town. Do you need anything?"

"Thanks, sweetie," Leonora said, smiling at her second child. "We're all set. Now don't you get too tired, honey." she added, gazing at Rose, who was eight months pregnant.

"I'm planning to take a nap before the party," Rose said.

"Good. Say hi to your parents and tell them we can't wait to see them tonight."

"Will do," Rose said, grasping Sam's arm as she stood.

"What a cute couple they are," Suzie said as the two headed for the house. "They remind me of you two at that age."

"Sam, maybe. He and his dad are both sweethearts, but Rosie's much nicer than I was."

"No such thing," her husband said, draping his arm around her as he winked at Spark. "So what's your prediction about your cook and the Miller lad?" he asked his friend.

"They were pretty cozy at breakfast, weren't they, Helen?"

Helen nodded. "They're a nice couple, and the Millers are a lovely family."

"I have no prediction," Spark said, "but I'd sure like to hire him. Not just to keep her here, but because he's a real firecracker."

"He gave a wonderful toast for his brother and Gailon Thursday night," Leonora said. "Very heartfelt and sweet."

"Yes," Helen said, nodding. "His parents were so proud."

CHAPTER 18

Ben sat in the wide chintz-covered easy chair in their bedroom, watching Leonora at her dressing table. She was applying the hint of makeup she always did for fancy occasions. Her deft touch meant that when she was finished, except for her lipstick, no one would know she wore anything. "Land sakes, you make a girl nervous watching me like that," she said, running the brush through her hair.

"You're just so pretty, can't help myself."

"Oh, pish tush! Don't you have to get ready too?"

He grinned. "Hair's combed, makeup's on, and it'll take me two shakes to hop into my suit."

Leonora gazed at her reflection and sighed.

"What's the matter, darlin'?" he asked, knowing a sigh meant distress of one sort or another. In forty years, he'd learned to pay attention to her sighs as they were often more accurate and telling than her words.

"You know, now that the day is here, I'm feeling kind of foolish about this party. I'm much happier planning special events for other people. Being the main attraction makes me very uncomfortable."

He rose and came close, arms circling around her, chin on her shoulder. "You've always been the main attraction to me. Always have, always will."

"That's different, and you know it."

He kissed the top of her head. "Just think of it as a party we're throwing for all the people we love, 'cause that's what it is. If we hadn't gotten hitched all those years ago, most of 'em wouldn't be here. That's something, isn't it?"

She smiled at his reflection in the mirror. "You're right, as always, my love, and didn't we have a fun wedding? Forty years. Where did they go?"

Ben dressed and went downstairs allowing her space. Another thing he'd learned after a lifetime together. His beautiful wife liked to primp and prep in private.

FULLY DRESSED AND READY FOR THE PARTY, BEN SAT IN THE LIVING room waiting for Leonora. As he sipped a glass of seltzer, he gazed out wide picture windows that looked out across the valley, remembering a smaller party forty years ago. They had it in Stanford at the small chapel where Spark and Patsy had been married. Their friends came, as well as Parker Brooks, Leonora's older brother. Since her parents refused to attend, Parker gave her away. Spark was best man and Suzie Miller, maid of honor. Patsy and their sorority sisters did the flowers and decorated the hall beside the chapel.

Leonora wore white crepe. The off-the-shoulder gown perfectly draped her slender body. He smiled, remembering the sexy side slit revealing just enough of her beautiful legs as she swished up the aisle. She carried calla lilies, and her blonde hair fell over her shoulders, held back by silver combs. She wore the pearl necklace he'd given her as an early Christmas present and matching pearl earrings. He had never seen anything so beautiful.

The day had been fun and relaxed, with dancing in the hall and delicious food provided by their friends. He knew she was disappointed that her parents refused to make the trip, but her lovely green eyes didn't show it as they gazed into his. Three days later, Lily and Thomas Brooks died in a plane crash.

"Ready, handsome?" she called from the hallway before stepping into the living room. "What do you think?"

"I think you'll put every woman there to shame."

"Thank you, but that's not what I'm asking. Does this look familiar?" She turned round and round, holding on to her skirt.

His mouth fell open. "Wow, that's not...?" The dress was now knee length, the slit only an inch or two, but it was the same dress.

"Yes it is. I had my seamstress cut it down and refit it."

"Well, you look more beautiful in it today than you did forty years ago."

"Not too dated?"

"Not a bit." He stood and came to hug her.

"Watch out, cowboy. You'll muss me!"

"All the better. It's our wedding night, after all."

She smiled, standing on tiptoe to kiss him. "Not till after the party. Now come on. Time to get cracking."

He cradled her in his arms. "I love you, darlin'."

"And I love you."

CHAPTER 19

"Here come the bride and groom now!" Ben Morgan cried as his parents stepped in the Lodge door. He and his siblings were the unofficial hosts for the evening, and all six of them stood by the door.

Leonora smiled at her offspring. "No fussing! Will you look at this. Jim and Bebe have added more decorations! Doesn't it look lovely?"

"Sure does," Spark said. Their dear friend stood at the opposite side of the door alongside his daughter Amy, son Buck and Helen and her daughters.

"Can't remember ever having a greeting party like this," Ben Senior said.

"Well, get used to it, Dad! We're just getting started," Kyle said, grinning.

Richard and Lucy Morgan followed his brother and sister-in-law in slapping Ben on the back and hugging Leonora. "Happy anniversary to the most loving couple on earth!"

"Come on, folks," Robbie said. "We're your escorts for the evening, and we've got some cool adventures planned."

"You better not have," his mother said. "Remember what we said. Just a nice party. No hijinks!"

"Yeah, right," her son Ben said. "Come on, follow your golden-haired boy."

Poster boards on easels trimmed with holiday garlands lined the room, displaying hundreds of photos of Ben and Leonora and their family. Three large screens at various spots streamed footage of old movies, still photos, and recent celebrations of events and the everyday life of the couple.

"How did you ever?" Leonora asked, leaning on Robbie's arm.

"It was a group effort. Mostly the women in the group."

Fires blazed in the mammoth stone hearths at the north and south ends of the room. As Leonora oohed and aahed at the photos and videos, Ben Senior stared above the south hearth mantel. "What's goin' on with the sheet?" he asked.

Ordinarily, a huge valley landscape hung over this mantelpiece, but the size of the frame underneath the sheet seemed a bit smaller. His parents turned to Robbie, who was grinning like the Cheshire Cat, his siblings right behind him.

Leonora followed her husband's gaze. "Oh dear. I hope nothing's happened to the DeCapo. That's a very valuable piece."

"Safely stored in back," Ruthie said, her eyes sparkling with excitement.

As she made a move toward the fireplace, Harley said, "Hey, babe, why not let Hope do the honors?"

"Of course," Ruthie said, stepping back to allow her shy sister-in-law to come forward.

Hope Seymour stepped from behind the others, smiling demurely. One of the region's most renowned painters, her landscapes hung all over the Southwest in homes, businesses and museums. Her work was sought after by collectors around the world. Robbie's wife was dressed in a long-sleeved peasant dress, white with blue and coral swirls of color, gathered at the waistline. Its plunging neckline shimmered with crystals that sparkled as she moved. It suited her perfectly. Her waist-length blonde was tied back in a long ponytail, delicate waves of curls framing her lovely face. When she reached the hearth, she crooked her finger at her husband, and he came forward to stand at the opposite side of the fireplace.

"Ready?" Robbie asked.

Hope nodded, and they each took hold of a corner of the sheet. As the sheet fell, a magnificent portrait of his father and mother was revealed. They stood arm in arm on the back terrace of the Big House, the valley and mountains behind them. The painting beautifully conveyed their love for each other.

"Oh, Hope, you didn't?" Leonora exclaimed.

"She did," her son Ben said. "Pretty spectacular, huh?" When he looked over and glimpsed tears rimming his father's eyes, he moved forward to embrace him. "Happy anniversary, Mom and Dad. We love you guys."

It was difficult to take one's eyes from the painting. Finally, Leonora sniffed. "Pish tush, my makeup's probably a mess!" She stood arm in arm with Maggie. "Should I go and touch up?"

"It's perfect. You look lovely," her daughter-in-law said.

Leonora turned to Hope. "I don't know what to say, sweetie. What an amazing gift."

Hope smiled, hugging her. "So glad you like it."

Leonora frowned. "Do we have to leave it here or can we take it home?"

"Your choice, Mom," Sam called as he and Kyle carried another draped frame from the coatroom.

Kyle paused as they set down their ends of the object. "We figured you might want to keep this one here since this is, after all, the Southwest equivalent of the Von Trapp Family Lodge."

"Whatever are you talking about?" she said, hand on hip, regarding her two sons.

Kyle laughed as he and Sam lifted the frame and removed the drape. "Behold the family Von Trapp. Oops, I mean the family Morgan!"

And there they were, Ben and Leonora surrounded by all six children and their families. The painting was from a photo had been taken the previous summer as they stood in roughly the same spot, on the terrace of the Big House, the valley backdrop behind them.

"Well, golly," Ben Senior said. "That's goin' home fer sure. If I can't have you all under the same roof, least we'll have this."

Leonora nodded. "It's lovely, Hope dear. I don't remember this photo where everyone looked terrific."

"That's because she used a number of pictures and a few actual sittings to paint it," Robbie said proudly.

"We never looked so good," his brother Ben said.

"Now how am I gonna get Hope back east to paint our family?" Richard Morgan asked. He had been standing at the back of the group, arm around Lucy, but now came forward to hug his brother and Leonora.

Hope smiled. "If you're serious, I'd love it when I have time. There's a lot I can do with photos first, so feel free to send any and all along."

"Let's get this party started," Robbie said. "These unveilings were supposed to take place after dinner, but since your eagle eyes spotted the sheet, what could we do? They're passing amazing food, champagne, and, of course, Norabens!"

His mother looked at him. "What in the world are you talking about?"

"A signature cocktail Jim asked the bartenders to create for this evening—Nora, Ben, get it?" Kyle said.

"And they're great. We've been sampling them all afternoon."

Leonora shook her head, a smile playing at the corners of her green eyes. "You all are too much. Thank you, thank you for everything!"

Beth Morgan Dillon hugged her parents, then reached for a tray of Norabens and grabbed two glasses. "You've got to at least try one. They're actually pretty good. Basically a Bloody Mary with lots of lime and cilantro."

"Yum," her mother said, taking a sip. "You look pretty tonight, baby."

And Beth did look pretty. The baby of the family, Ruthie was petite and all curves, while their older daughter was tall and slender. She wore a cranberry velvet skirt and cream-colored blouse, a long single strand of pearls, and teardrop earrings. Her straight brown hair was held back by a thin velvet headband the same color as her skirt. Beth leaned toward her mother's ear. "Pastor Jane is here if you'd like to quietly renew your vows during the evening."

Her mother reached up and touched her cheek. "Tempting offer, honey, but your father and I did that in private this afternoon. Maybe at our fiftieth?"

"Hey, these Norabens are pretty good," Ben Senior said, raising his glass in a toast.

"Well, enjoy it, 'cause that's your last one," Leonora said, clinking her glass against his. "Now I'm ready to mingle with my sweetheart."

CHAPTER 20

"Our parents are hard acts to follow, aren't they?" Karen Miller said as she and Weezie Morgan watched Rex and Faith Miller dancing, Richard and Lucy Morgan not far away.

Weezie nodded. "Never mind this bunch. Start at the top with the anniversary couple and go right on down the line. I wonder if I'll ever get on the love train?"

Karen nudged her. "Don't look now, but there's a really cute cowboy eyeing you. Wait, he's coming our way."

"Hey, ladies." The young, craggy-faced cowboy with shoulder-length dirty-blonde hair, beard, and mustache, tilted his head, looking at Weezie.

"Hey, yourself," Karen said.

"I'm Whip... Whip Kittredge. Care to dance?" As he spoke, he extended his hand to Weezie.

"Sure, of course," she sputtered, taking his hand. With a quick backward glance at Karen, Weezie followed Whip to the dance floor.

When they found an open spot, he pulled her into his arms. "This okay?"

She nodded.

"You're one of the East Coast Morgans, aren't you?"

"Guilty," she said, gazing into his smoky-gray eyes. "I'm the youngest of the East Coast Morgans. Weezie."

"That's an unusual name. Pretty." *And she sure is pretty with her short brown hair and those chocolate eyes dancing with light.*

"Short for Louise. I was named after my aunt. Do you work here on the ranch?"

"Valley Stables."

"Oh? I don't remember seeing you when we were here last year. What do you do?"

"That was probably when I was away. Went home to get knee surgery."

"Yuck."

"Yup. Horse reared, then fell on me. Wasn't pretty. To answer your question, I'm one of the wranglers and stable hands. I do whatever needs to be done. My favorite job is exercising the horses."

"Me too."

"You work on a ranch?"

Weezie nodded. "My dad's farm. We're actually doing a lot of the same things you are. I work with Gus Casey. Did you know him?"

"Sure did. We miss ole Gus."

Whip was a great dancer, and as the music picked up, he twirled her around the dance floor, never missing a beat. Weezie felt warm and safe in his arms. She closed her eyes and gave herself over to his lead. The reel ended, and the band started playing Clapton's "Wonderful Tonight." He pulled her a little closer, not bothering to ask if she wanted to dance again. Her dreamy smile and closed eyes were answer enough.

"Uh-oh," Pam Morgan said, standing beside her sister Gail, Harriet, and Aria. "Weezie's found a cowboy. Who is he? Do we know?"

Aria followed her gaze. "That's Whip Kittredge. Works out at the stables. I chased him for months, but he never gave me the time of day."

Gail smiled. "Thank goodness. If you were with him, you'd have never met my brother-in-law!"

"Where is Jonas tonight?" Pam asked. "I haven't seen that gorgeous fellow all night."

Aria shrugged. "Don't think I haven't noticed his absence. He's been on the terrace talking with Spark and his son. And you all leave tomorrow!"

"Yes, but Jonas travels constantly. If he's on the West Coast, he can always stop in to see everyone here, and I suspect he will," Gail said.

"Here comes your hunky husband," Aria said. "Yours too," she added, giving Pam a look.

"Boyfriend," Pam said, smiling as she took Sandy's hand and allowed him to lead her away.

"Fiancé," Gail called after her as Tim Miller grabbed his wife and headed out to the floor.

"Don't you leave me too," Aria said to Harriet. The women had become good friends on Harriet's visits, one of the few friends Aria had outside of work. "Where's Kyle anyway?"

"I think he's with his brothers plotting one last something for their parents."

"Weren't the toasts touching?" Aria said. "You are so lucky to come from such loving families. I had nothing like that growing up."

Harriet patted her hand. She knew a bit about Aria's past. Alcoholic father who left when she was young, mother married four times, every husband a bigger loser than the previous one. She had a sister, but they weren't close. Spark Foster and his clan were the nearest thing to family she'd ever had. "Yes, they were very touching. Those Morgan guys are charmers, aren't they?"

"Starting with Ben Senior. Don't forget his college buddy. Spark's speech might have been my favorite," Aria said.

"Mine too. Uh-oh, I see the guys coming in now."

"No Jonas, though," Aria said, disappointment in her tone.

The dance ended, and as they watched, Ben Morgan, the son, stepped up and took the mic. "No worries folks," he said, grinning from ear to ear. "This is the last time you'll have to listen to me tonight. Promise. The family Morgan wanted to end with a window into the amazing life of our parents. So here is our version of Ben and Leonora, the first forty years."

Two chairs were placed at the end of the crowd, and Sam led his parents to them. Then all the Morgan siblings as well as Maggie and Emma came forward. For the next twenty minutes, they presented a hilarious skit beginning with Ben and Leonora's meeting at Stanford and ending with their entrance earlier in the evening. Ruthie played her mother with a silly blonde wig, Beth various roles as the women in her life, including Suzie Miller and some of her Cowbelle friends. Maggie played Carmela as the long-suffering housekeeper, as well as the sisters and herself at various points. Ben played his father, Robbie, and Spark Foster. Sam and Kyle played the brothers as well as whatever part was needed for a particular scene. Laughter echoed through the tent as Ben and Leonora's life unfolded.

They concluded with the couple stepping through the door of the Lodge. Leonora shook her head. "You devils. We'll get you for this!"

"Not if you're not here," Beth said, stepping forward and handing them an envelope.

Leonora gave it to her husband. "You open it. I don't think I can handle any more surprises tonight."

"They're sending us to London, darlin'. And the Lakes."

Arm around his wife, Ben said, "Mags and I loved our trip there and thought you should see it."

"This is too much," Leonora said. "Much too much."

"Well, you're going, 'cause if you don't, you'll have some really disappointed grandchildren."

"Not to mention your buddies," Spark said, standing tall at the back of the crowd.

"What're you talkin' about, ole man?" Ben Senior asked, grinning at his friend and knowing full well what was coming.

"Don't forget your brother," Richard called.

Kyle nodded, smiling at his parents. "We've rented five cottages in Grasmere and have taken over an entire floor of our London hotel. You didn't think we'd let ya go alone, did ya?"

"Why, you little stinkers!" Leonora said, rising stiffly with Ben's help, hugging each of her children and their spouses in turn.

Emma jumped into her grandfather's arms. "Aren't you excited, Grandpa?"

"More excited then you'll ever know, honey. Did you know about this?"

"Sure did." Arms round his neck, she leaned close to his ear. "But we didn't tell Bennie 'cause he's a blabbermouth."

CHAPTER 21

"So how cool is that?" Jonas said as he came to stand next to Aria. Startled, Aria turned violet eyes to him. "Oh, hello. Yes, very cool. Wish I was going."

"Maybe you are."

"I doubt it."

"Some day?"

She shrugged. "Haven't seen much of you tonight."

"Yeah, I've been distracted. Think they'll start playing again? I'd love a dance."

"Not if it ends like our last one," she said.

"Come on, one dance can't hurt."

He held out his hand, and she took it, sensation coursing through her body like lightning. *Big mistake!* she thought as they walked into the throng of dancers.

"You okay?" he asked as he drew her into his arms.

Eyes sad, she gazed up at his. "Define okay."

"Listen, Aria. Last night was incredible. Beyond incredible, in fact. I'm sorry I can't give more right now."

She felt him grow hard against her belly and moved back, breaking contact. "The story of my life."

"Don't say that. It wasn't just sex for me. My life's just really messed up right now. I'd like to keep in touch even if I can't promise any more."

"I understand. I do. I was a full participant last night. No worries."

His smile as he looked down melted her heart and Aria fought to hold back tears. "Friends?" he said softly.

"Friends," she whispered, resting her head on his chest for just a moment as the song wound down.

As another song started, this one fast and peppy, she said, "Would you excuse me? I think I'm going to take off. I have a bit of a headache, and I've got a big send-off breakfast to start for Spark's guests."

Before he could stop her, Aria slipped into the crowd and disappeared.

His sister Karen found him at the edge of the dance floor. "Another broken heart at the hands of Jonas Miller?"

"You're one to talk. I saw you with Rich Morgan. Poor guy won't know what hit him when you tell him adios."

"Ha-ha. We're just friends."

"Yeah, right. Have you told him that?"

"No, but I'm gonna. Now what's up with you and the chef?"

"Nothing. We had a moment, but it's passed and it's time to go home."

"For you, maybe, but I'd love another few weeks out here. Even with the sprinkling of snow they had this morning, I could get used to this weather."

"Don't look now, but your friend is headed this way," he said as Rich approached. "Least you get to take your friend home."

"Very funny," Karen said as she turned and smiled at Rich.

"One more?" he said. "They tell me the band is leaving soon." The eldest of the East Coast Morgans, Rich was slender and good-looking, with his father's trademark bushy eyebrows. His green eyes were warm, and he had an endearing habit of brushing strands of his straight hair from his forehead, even when the gesture was unnecessary.

Karen smiled, holding out her hand. "I'd love to."

As he drew her close, her libido surged and her breath grew rapid. "Why, Mr. Morgan, I'd better be careful you don't sweep me off my feet."

Rich grinned, his eyes communicating more than they should. "That's the general idea."

Why not? she thought, moving closer to nuzzle his neck. *Rich Morgan is steady, stable, and caring. I could do worse.*

"WELL, MY BRIDE. THINK WE CAN BLOW THIS POP STAND AND START OUR wedding night?" Ben asked, arm around Leonora as they watched their family and friends.

"Pop stand? Where do you get these expressions?"

He grinned, kissing the top of her head. "The kids, of course."

She leaned against him, drawing strength and support from his warm, familiar presence. "Sammie just told me the band's playing two more songs and that's it. We can sneak out after that."

"What a night, huh?"

She shook her head, a happy smile on her face. "Those kids. They...they shouldn't have." Her voice cracked as she wiped back tears.

"We're damn lucky, that's for sure."

"Yes, we are. Look," she said, gazing at the dance floor. "Several new romances blooming out there."

"Oh?"

"Well, there's our nephew and Karen Miller. They make a cute couple, even though the word on her is that she's a bit of a flibbertigibbet. Apparently, she's left a few men at the altar."

"You don't say. That cute little gal?"

"Cute little gal my eye. More like a vixen, but she's is Harriet's best friend, so she must have some redeeming qualities."

"Nora Morgan," he said, voice full of mock reproach. "I thought you told me you were turning over a new leaf."

"Oh pish tush."

"So what other romantic liaisons have you uncovered?"

"Well, there's the Miller boy and Aria. Spark would horsewhip him if he tried to lure her east."

"Naw. Her happiness would trump his stomach if I know my buddy."

"You're right, of course. Dear Spark. He and Helen get on so well. I still wonder if that spark might grow. It would be lovely to have her here, at least part of the year. We've grown quite close."

"You never know."

Leonora turned her sharp green eyes to his. "Do you know something? If you do, you'd better tell me!"

Ben laughed, hugging her. "I know nothing except no one will ever replace his Patsy or her late husband."

"No one's asking for that. Just for them to be happy surrounded by their friends."

"And she has a passel back in Horseshoe Crab Cove."

Leonora nodded. "I know, I know. Those Yarners. I envy her them."

"You've got your Cowbelles."

She shook her head. "Not the same. I love 'em all, but they're not what I'd call close friends. Those are rare and precious, like dear Suzie and Spark and Patsy."

As the band announced their last song and strands of "My Girl" began, Ben took her hand. "Come on, darlin'. They're playin' our song."

As he drew her close, Leonora sighed. "I love you."

"Right back atcha, darlin'. Love you so much, I'm afraid my heart'll bust."

"Ben Morgan, you are a charmer, but don't you dare bust your heart over me," she said, resting her head against his strong, familiar chest.

CHAPTER 22

The Easterners departed early, shuttled to Grenville Airport in one of Spark's SUVs. Harriet's father and stepmother had departed Sunday on a commercial flight, but Spark's plane and two additional charter flights organized by him flew everyone else eastward. Jonas and Aria did not meet again, and Karen and Rich flew back on separate planes, so the romantic liaisons seemed to have cooled. Harriet and Kyle and Sam and Rose were staying for Christmas.

In the aftermath of goodbyes, Ben, Leonora, Sam, Rose, Kyle, and Harriet sat chatting in the Big House living room, tea, hot chocolate, or, in Sam and Kyle's case, beers in hand. The room was a Christmas wonderland, a sea of red and green, with gold and silver accents. "What a week," Harriet said, sipping the best hot chocolate she'd ever tasted.

Leonora smiled at her daughter-in-law. "Sure was. I wish your mom could've stayed for Christmas."

"Me too. She was torn, but the grandkids and her Darn Yarners won out."

"I was just saying to Ben how much I envy her that group of friends."

"They've been pretty special to her and to us."

"Like Spark," Kyle said. "They're family."

His father smiled. "We're a pretty lucky bunch. When are you kids takin' off?" he asked, turning to Sam and Rose, who were moving to her parents' home for the rest of their stay.

She smiled at the father-in-law, whom she loved so dearly. Perhaps even more than her own father lost to alcoholism years ago. "I promised Mom we'd be there for dinner. Lang, Beth, and Lily are coming."

"How fun."

Rose touched her pregnant belly. "Truthfully, I'd rather have a quick sandwich, put my feet up, and go to bed early. I'm sure Sam would too."

"We'll soldier on for Martha," Sam said, setting his empty beer mug on a colorful Christmas coaster.

Leonora frowned. "I know you will. Poor Martha. We missed her at all the events this week. After Christmas, I'm going to drag her to lunch and share photos and highlights."

"I know she'd love it," Rose said. "She really wanted to come, especially last night, but it's hard to leave him."

"Of course it is," Leonora said.

"Is it just us for dinner tonight?" Kyle asked. "We could even take you guys out to the Bulldog."

"Great idea!" his father said.

Leonora frowned. "As appealing as that sounds, Robbie and Hope are coming, as well as Ruthie, Harley, Charlotte, and Willow. Poor Willow must be exhausted after all the babysitting she's done the past few days." Harley's nineteen-year-old daughter lived with her father and Ruthie when she wasn't in school. She also worked at the Cottage, the ranch's day care facility, and was a frequent and beloved babysitter for the ranch's growing number of children.

"She's tough and strong," Kyle said.

"That she is," his father said, slapping his knee.

"What about Ben and Mags?" Kyle asked.

Leonora winked at her son. "They're going to Ned's. Apparently, he's been squiring the town's new acupuncturist around, and he wants them to meet her."

"Why didn't he bring her to the wedding?" Sam asked.

Leonora set down her empty mug. "She was away at a conference. She was presenting, or she would have canceled."

Sam raised his eyebrow. "And you know this because?"

"Well, if you must know, I've been seeing her to deal with some leg pain. She's very nice. Name's Wrenn Parsons. I'd guess she's in her mid to late forties. Tall and pretty."

"What kind of leg pain?" Sam asked.

Leonora looked at her husband. He smiled, reaching over to take her hand. "Tell 'em, honey. You were gonna do it at dinner anyway."

"Tell us what?" Kyle said.

Leonora raised her hands. "It's nothing major. I've been having some leg pain and have slowly lost range of motion in my legs. I love my Misty, but I couldn't ride right now if I tried. Anyway, I tried acupuncture, physical therapy, and a bunch of other things, but the doctors tell me I need new hips."

"When?" Sam asked.

"Right after the new year. My surgery is scheduled for January sixth if I can get in all the other appointments leading up to it!"

"What can we do, Mom?" Sam asked. "Rose has to go back, but I could stay on."

"We can too," Harriet said. "I could get someone to cover my classes."

"Absolutely not! You are wonderful chickens to offer, but we have plenty of help around here. They tell us it's not a bad recovery."

Rose nodded. "Yes, much easier recovery than knees. And they have so many new techniques now. Much less traumatic."

"Still enough trauma for me. Having the top of my thigh bone cut off and a metal thingamajig popped in... There's really no alternative unless I want to be hobbling and crippled within the next few years. Anyway, enough about me. Wrenn is lovely, and I think she and Ned could be very compatible."

"That's nice for him," Harriet said. "He's such a great guy."

Leonora nodded. "He's the one who should be having hip replacements, for goodness sakes. After all his bucking and flying through the air!" The most famous wrangler the Valley had ever produced, Maggie's dad was retired now, but he had ridden in hundreds of rodeos over the years.

"You're going to do just fine Mom," Sam said. "Piece of cake."

His mother gave him a wry smile. "Easy for you to say."

CHAPTER 23

Spark's mansion was aglow with lights and colorful Christmas decorations in every room thanks to Aria and his daughter Amy's collaboration. There were three trees, each with a different theme in the huge great room, dining room, and Spark's library. The smallest, in the library, was an upside-down tree decorated in wild stripes and tinsel. The largest, in the living room, was traditional, all golds, reds, and greens. The dining room tree was a white Christmas theme in silver and white.

"And I thought my in-laws overdid things," Harriet said, gazing at the dining room tree, then the long table set for Christmas Eve dinner.

"Spark loves Christmas," Aria said.

Harriet laughed. "I can see that. Just as well that Mom went home. She favors simple. Handmade decorations and not too many of them."

Aria forced a smile. "Well, you know Spark. He never does anything halfway. He's even got Santa coming later for the kids."

"No!"

"Yup. Roped Mickey into it, poor guy." She referred to Spark's pilot, whom they all knew well from flights back and forth across the country.

"You okay?" Harriet asked, gazing at her friend. "You look a little glum."

Aria shrugged. "Story of my life. Every time I meet a guy, he runs in the other direction."

"How did you and Jonas leave things?"

"Goodbye, see you again someday." Her eyes filled with tears as she hopped up. "Sorry I've gotta get back to the kitchen. See you later, okay?"

Harriet watched the beautiful chef dressed in her crisp white coat disappear through the kitchen doors.

"Hey, babe. Here you are. I was wondering where you'd gotten to. Why the long face?" Kyle put his arm around her, kissing her cheek.

"I just feel bad for Aria with Jonas leaving and all."

"Did she scare him off?" Kyle asked. While his wife and Aria had become good friends, he was not as enamored of Spark's chef. There had been one particular night when Aria's relentless pursuit of him had left a bad taste.

Harriet elbowed him. "Not funny."

"Hey, you two," Leonora said, strolling into the room. "Why are you hiding in here? Oh my, doesn't Spark's table look magical?" And it did. In keeping with the tree, the table was all silver and white, from the row of highly polished candlesticks to the crisp white linens and silver-lined china.

Kyle rolled his eyes. "We're not hiding."

"Well then, come into the great room with the rest of us. Harriet, I didn't tell you as we were leaving. That dress is spectacular on you."

Harriet blushed. "Thanks, Leonora. It's new. Aria helped me pick it out at Gabriela's." A soft moss green velvet, the dress followed the beautiful contours of her slender frame, its neck revealing just a hint of cleavage. The full and flouncy skirt fell just above her knees, and she wore simple gray pumps.

"I should have known. Gabriela has amazing clothes and she knows just what works! It really suits you. I broke down and tried her this fall. In fact, this little number came from her. I almost never wear black, but I adore it. So does Ben."

"It's lovely," Harriet said, but then her mother-in-law always looked lovely. Tonight she was in black, a long-sleeved ruched viscose crepe pencil dress with high neck accented with simple gold jewelry and black pumps.

As they followed Kyle's mother into the great room, Kyle drew her close. "Sure does suit you, sweetheart."

For an instant, Harriet rested her head on his shoulder. "A nice change from my usual pioneer woman attire?"

He leaned over and kissed her temple. "Don't know what you mean."

"Yes, you do, but I love you for saying that."

"You always look gorgeous to me."

"Well, don't you put the sun to shame?" Spark said, greeting them. "Two of the prettiest ladies I know. What can I get you to drink?"

Both Harriet and Leonora requested white wine, and the men headed to the bar.

"What a sweetheart Spark is," Harriet said.

Leonora nodded. "He's a peach. And he's been with Ben and me through thick and thin."

"Well, he's sure been wonderful to Mom and me. Brought her out of her shell and made her smile."

"Think they'll ever...?" Leonora asked, leaving the words unsaid.

Harriet smiled. "Who knows. I think this may be all Mom can give. She loved Tim with all her heart and had him for just the blink of an eye. So unfair after all those years with Dad."

Leonora's arm circled her daughter-in-law's waist, hugging her. "We're so glad you're here. I'm sure it was hard not being with your family."

"You're my family too. We'll ring in the new year with them."

"At Richard and Lucy's?"

Harriet shook her head. "Clara and Will wanted to do it this year, so we'll all go there."

"What fun, darlin'."

As the men came back with their wine, Harriet said, "Do you miss Beth and Sam tonight?"

"No, we get 'em tomorrow. So nice for Martha and Jaybo to have them tonight. Poor Martha is so housebound. He won't go anywhere, and she won't leave him. Fortunately, their loving children and grandbaby keep her smiling."

"And another one on the way," Harriet said, as Kyle handed her the wineglass.

"Another what?" he asked.

"Baby. Our newest grandbaby, of course!" Leonora said as her husband approached, complimenting Harriet's dress and forestalling any questions about their future plans for children.

As Harriet and Kyle strolled off to join Maggie and Ben, Ben Senior hugged her. "Good girl."

"What're you on about?"

"No mentioning grandkids. Not to those two or Hope and Robbie."

"Oh pish tush! I can dream, can't I?"

"Well, since Hope can't have kids, that dream's goin' nowhere, my love. And who knows what Kyle and Harriet have planned." After a botched abortion, Robbie's wife had undergone an emergency hysterectomy that had saved her life. Thus far, the couple refused to discuss adoption.

"I know, I know. I just want everyone to be happy."

He leaned down and kissed her forehead. "Of course you do. That's why I love you so much."

CHAPTER 24

Aria had made cioppino, Spark's traditional Christmas Eve meal. The hearty fisherman's stew was brimming with lobster, mussels, clams, fennel, shallots, scallops, and chunks of red snapper, all flown in from the West Coast. There were baskets of thick crusty bread to soak up a savory red sauce infused with saffron and other spices. A colorful green salad followed, the lettuces and bright nasturtium flowers picked that morning at the farm at Morgan's Run.

Buck Foster groaned with pleasure as he took a bite of bread. "I dream of this meal all year long. So incredible."

Aria, who, after serving, had joined them at the table and sat across from Spark's son, said, "You know, you only have to ask. With a few days' notice, I can whip this up any time."

Buck smiled. "I know, but half the pleasure is the anticipation. So what's Santa bringing my favorite nephew?" he asked, winking at Toby, who sat between his parents. Toby smiled but said nothing.

"Now that would spoil the surprise," Jeb said, ruffling his son's blond curls.

"After dinner, Grampa says we can all open one present," Emma said. "If you're good," she added, frowning at her brother, who had slipped out of his seat and under the table.

Maggie gave her husband a look that sent him under the table in pursuit. "I'm sorry, Spark."

From the far end of the table, the host grinned. "Not a bit of it. Love every minute of their shenanigans." He winked at Maggie. "Although I'm not sure if people under the table will get dessert."

Instantly, a curly brown head popped up and slid back into his seat. Ben the third spent the next ten minutes playing with his french fries and eating bits of burger. When Maggie, Amy, and Aria rose to clear the table, he hopped down again, but this time, his father intercepted him. "Not so fast, buddy!"

For years, Patsy Foster had collected antique ice-cream molds. There were molds for many holidays, but her favorite were the Christmas ones in the shape of candles, wreaths, trees, and candy canes. Aria's homemade ice cream made each creation extra special. Truly works of art, she served them on exquisite Spode Christmas plates. Many oohs and aahs accompanied the presentation. Small pitchers of rich chocolate sauce were passed, as well as platters of colorful Christmas cookies.

As Harriet passed a cookie platter to Kyle, she said, "These are beautiful, Aria. You must have been baking for months."

Aria nodded. "Since right after Thanksgiving. My favorite kind of baking."

Harriet smiled. "We used to love to make Christmas cookies with our mom. Was that your bread too? It was perfect."

"Nope. I like to make bread, but I could never come close to what the Café does. It's not Portland sourdough, but it's pretty darn close."

Seated beside her beloved grandfather, Emma carefully spooned small bites of her ice-cream wreath while her brother's candy cane slipped around his plate as he attempted to chop it with his spoon. Maggie waved at her husband. "Cut it up before it goes flying into the air. In fact, would it be okay if we got a bowl for him?"

Aria popped up. "I'll get one. They're right here." She grabbed a matching Spode bowl from the sideboard and deftly transferred the candy cane into it. "Here, buddy, let me fix it for you," she said, taking his spoon and cutting the cane in pieces.

The child frowned, grabbed a gingerbread man from the platter, jumped down from his seat, and ran toward the great room and its twenty-foot tree.

"Ben!" Maggie cried.

"Let him go," Spark said. "He can't get into too much trouble."

"Wanna bet?" his father said.

Willow hopped up. "I'll go watch him. No worries."

"Thanks, honey," Harley said, smiling at his daughter.

"Take your ice cream with you, sweetie," Spark said as Aria stood and went to the sideboard, slipping the remains of Willow's chocolate reindeer into a bowl. She followed Willow into the great room, then returned and sat down.

"Truth is," the chef said, "these look pretty, but they're not that popular with kids. I suspect they'd rather have bubble gum ice cream."

"On the menu for next year, then!" Spark said.

"I love mine!" Emma said, holding up a spoonful of ice cream.

"But you're an angel," Aria said. "You and Toby are both angels."

Shortly after the group assembled in the great room. Amy played the piano, and they sang a few favorite carols. Ben held his wriggling son during the singing as Maggie and Emma stood together holding hands, her father, Ned, beside them. When the group completed a rousing rendition of "Jingle Bells," sleigh bells sounded from the front hall, accompanied by a hearty "Ho, ho, ho!"

Charlotte buried her face in her father's shoulder as Ben the third screamed and wriggled out of his father's arms. "Santa!"

Spark's pilot, Mickey, made a jolly Santa, dressed in red velvet and sporting a long white beard.

"Oh my, he's perfect, Spark," Leonora whispered. "Is he still willing to make a brief appearance tomorrow so Lily will see him?"

"Sure is. Then I've released him till the new year. He'll take the plane and fly home to Portland to be with his family."

"You really are the most wonderful man, Spark Foster," she said, hugging him.

"And you two are the dearest friends a man could ever want. In the words of the immortal Tiny Tim—God bless us, every one!"

"I believe those were Scrooge's words," Leonora said. "But who cares. We love them and you anyway!"

CHAPTER 25

Christmas Day, the family started spilling in midmorning. Overcoats over pajamas, they shed outer garments and congregated in the dining room for Carmela's brunch of Southwestern eggs benedict, the hollandaise laced with cilantro and chilis. The long table was stretched to its limit with twenty diners. For the midafternoon Christmas dinner, which would include Spark's family, the Dillons, and Carmela and Raoul, the kids and some adults would be at separate tables in the adjacent living room. Now, everyone fit, and the conversation was lively as Christmas crackers popped and everyone donned paper hats and chatted about the evening's snowfall and the day ahead.

"If it's still on the ground, Mags and I are gonna take the kids sledding at Molson's Ridge," Ben said. "Anyone want to join us?"

"We're in," Harley said.

"Count Lily and me in too," Lang said. "I'm guessing Beth would rather nap before the feast."

His wife nodded. Five months pregnant, she was having a hard time with sleeping and continued bouts of morning sickness. "You guessed right."

"I'm sure Amy and Jeb will want to bring Toby," Maggie said. "It'll be fun if the snow doesn't melt before then."

"How was your time last night at Spark's?" Lang asked.

Maggie smiled at her brother-in-law. "You know Spark. Amazing food, beautiful decorations, over-the-top everything! And a visit from you-know-who." She winked at Beth and Lang. "Rumor has it a certain someone might make a second appearance today."

"How was your dinner with Martha and Jaybo?" Leonora asked.

"Very nice. Quiet," Beth said.

"Quiet is good," Lang said, a frown creasing his handsome face.

"How's your dad feeling?"

"Okay," Rose said. "He's hoping to come this afternoon."

As talk drifted on and conversations scattered the length of the table, Lang turned to Ben and Maggie. "Truth? Last night was a horror show. Rose and I are hoping Mom will agree to come alone today and leave the old drunk to stew by himself."

Maggie gazed across at him. "Oh, I'm so sorry. So hard on all of you."

"And Lily had to miss Santa and her cousins."

Beth shook her head. "Shush. She doesn't know the difference, and she's happy as a clam today. Anyway, last night was about your mom, not him."

After breakfast, they gathered around the tree for stockings. The adults drew names, and each filled another adult's stocking and Leonora and Ben filled the children's stockings. Most of the adult gifts were silly, and then the guessing game began to determine who had filled whose stocking. When the raucous opening was over, the kids played with their little toys and the adults sat back, sated and happy with mugs of cider, coffee, hot chocolate, and tea. Shortly after noon, the group dispersed and everyone gathered things to go home. The sledders made plans to meet at the stables for the short wagon ride to Molson's Ridge.

"Be careful!" Leonora said, hugging Emma at the door. "Don't let your dad do any crazy stunts."

Emma smiled, hugging her grandmother. "Don't worry, Grandma. I'll watch him and Bennie too."

"Don't we know it!" her grandfather said, swooping her up in his arms and kissing her. The family patriarch and his sweet, gentle granddaughter had a special relationship. Ever since she was four and the day he realized she was his, Ben Senior was smitten, as was the little girl with curly dark hair so like her dad's. In fact, he and Ruthie had guessed the connection long before the rest of the family, including his son, Ben, Emma's father.

"Go on now, precious," Leonora said, "before your grandpa decides to join you and I have to put my foot down."

SLEDDING AT MOLSON'S RIDGE INVOLVED PILING SLEDS AND PEOPLE into the farm wagon, pulled by two of the stable horses. Then they scaled the craggy rise, hopped on toboggans, saucers, and sleds and sailed down onto the snow-covered meadow below. Buck Foster waited at the bottom to help sledders stay on course, then brush off and regroup before the climb back up the rise. "I give us three, maybe four runs, and the snow will be history," Ben said as he hopped on a toboggan behind his son and daughter.

Maggie gave them a push, then helped push Lang and Lily off on a bright red saucer. "Be careful that thing doesn't land you in a clump of sagebrush," she called as Lang whooped, holding his daughter tight.

Next, Jeb shoved off with Toby as Amy stood watching with Maggie. Harley gave Ruthie and Charlotte a push on his old Radio Flyer, then shook his head. "That woman'll be the death of me."

Amy laughed. "Not on that thing. They'll be lucky if they don't stick in the mud halfway down the hill."

Harley grinned. "Serve her right. How's she think they're getting that back up?" he said as he began climbing down the side path to the meadow.

"Who would have thought two women could turn my old boss into the biggest softie this side of the Rockies?" Maggie said, smiling as she watched the tall wrangler's descent.

"Love'll do that," Amy said, her arm circling Maggie's waist. "We're a lucky bunch, aren't we?"

"Sure are." Maggie watched her husband wrestling the toboggan and their son back up the path. "How was breakfast at your Dad's?"

"Ridiculously over-the-top as always."

"I was thinking Jeb's mom and dad might have come for Christmas. Didn't they come last year?"

"Yes, but we spent Thanksgiving in Flagstaff, so they decided to celebrate with his sisters' families. They may come for New Year's. In truth, I think they get a bit overwhelmed at Dad's house."

"Don't they stay with you?"

"Yes, but you know Dad. He wants to entertain everyone every second of the day and night, and he has the means and the staff to do it."

Maggie laughed. "Join the club! I don't know how they'll fit everyone in the Big House this year, but it will be a wild afternoon. My dad's bringing Wrenn. Poor woman won't know what hit her."

"That's right, they're dating, huh?" Amy said, keeping an eye on Jeb, who held Toby as he pulled their small toboggan up the path.

"Yup."

"She's a nice person."

Maggie nodded. "Yes, she is."

"I went to her a few months ago when I hurt my back."

"Oh?"

"It really helped. I'm a firm believer in acupuncture."

"Me too."

"How's it going with her and your dad?"

Maggie smiled. "He's pretty smitten. Haven't seen this side of him ever."

"Well, good for him," Amy said.

Ben and the kids reached them. "Your turn, Mama," he said, waving Maggie onto the toboggan.

The kids jumped on, squealing, "Come on, Mommy!" in unison.

Maggie shook her head, giving her husband a look as she slipped on behind Bennie. "Okay, but only if after you give us a push, you hightail it down to the bottom to help with you-know-who."

"You got it, babe." He took a running start and let go as the toboggan hurtled down the slope.

The kids screamed, and Maggie cried, "I'll get you for this, Ben Morgan!"

CHAPTER 26

Along with all the other holiday and party preparations, Carmela had been cooking for weeks preparing Christmas dinner. Raoul barbequed ranch-raised geese on a slow-turning spit, and she served platters of side dishes from mashed potatoes, roasted portabella mushrooms, nut-and-seed burgers, cauliflower steaks, salads, roasted vegetables, and platters of breads.

The meal began with lobster bisque flown in from New England, a gift from Richard Morgan to his brother's family. The sublime creamy soup was brimming with chunks of fresh lobster meat, a hint of fine sherry finishing it off. Carmela served crusty bread and flavored olive oils on the side.

Kyle groaned as he took a spoonful. "Geez, where did Uncle Dick get this? It's amazing. I sure haven't tasted anything like this on the East Coast."

Ben Senior grinned. "Apparently, his cook, Callie, makes it for their Christmas dinner. It's the only time of year she serves it, although Richard told me if he begs, she'll agree to freeze a few gallons for him."

"Well, I'm gonna start hounding her as soon as we get home," Kyle said, "'cause we've gotta have the recipe."

Harriet patted his hand. "Good luck with that. From what I hear, Callie guards the recipe as if her life depended on it."

Aria set down her spoon. "I betcha I could experiment and eventually duplicate it. Maybe if I ever get east, I'll sneak one of the frozen batches and borrow a kitchen."

"Oh pish tush," Leonora said. "Let's just enjoy this once-in-a-lifetime treat and let poor Callie keep her secrets." Then, seeing Aria's face fall, she winked at Spark's chef. "Even though I'm certain you could easily crack the code, darlin'."

"So how was the sleddin' today?" Spark asked. "My crew hasn't had a second to fill me in."

Buck raised his wineglass. "Your intrepid son may have frost bite on his toes after playing search and rescue officer all afternoon."

Eyes wide, Maggie stared at him. "You're kidding, right?"

"Yes, he is," Amy, his sister, said. "Always been the biggest baby."

"He catched me and Mommy," Bennie said, waving french fries in each hand as he sat between Toby and his sister at the children's table.

"Sure did," Maggie said. "No thanks to your father, who sent us down the hill at a hundred miles an hour."

"Amazin' to think we had enough snow for you to go at all," Spark said.

"It was a blast," Ruthie said. "The first white Christmas we've had in ages."

"I'm glad my sweet grandchildren returned in one piece," Leonora said, waving at Lily from across the room before turning to Wrenn Parsons, seated next to Maggie's dad, Ned. "Do you have children, Wrenn?"

"No. I wish," she said. Wraith thin and tall, with shoulder length salt-and-pepper hair, she wore a lovely red peasant style dress, lacy and trimmed with velvet. It suited her, bringing out the rosiness of her angular cheeks. Not exactly beautiful, the forty-something acupuncturist was what one might call handsome. Her smile lit up the room.

~

By the time Carmela announced that desserts were on the sideboard, everyone was sated with great food, incredible wines, and the warmth of dining with loved ones. "Come on, wife of mine," Kyle said, standing and offering Harriet his hand. "You're about to witness one of the miracles of Christmas—Carmela's bevy of Buche de Noels."

The sideboard held four yule logs, one labeled vegan. Between each Buche de Noel sat bowls of whipped cream, pitchers of dark chocolate sauces and platters of Christmas cookies.

"Oh my goodness!" Harriet said. "Which one do you recommend?"

Her father in law patted her shoulder. "Sometimes we sample them all, honey!"

Carmela served the children ice-cream sundaes with cones on top decorated like small pointy-hatted elves. Maggie and Beth carved slices of Buche de Noel as Raoul served coffees and teas. As was tradition, he and Carmela joined the family for dessert.

Halfway through his ice cream, Ben the third hopped down and came to sit on his father's lap. Ben kissed the top of his head. "You're a tired cowboy, aren't you?"

"He's still our little napper, if we let him," Maggie said.

"But then he's up till midnight," Ben said.

"I wish Charlotte would nap at least on the weekends," Ruthie said. "'Cause I'd sure love a nap."

Rose had been quietly listening to the conversation. "How about Lily?" she asked.

"Lily's a champion napper," Lang said. "Just ask 'em at the Cottage. They always have to wake her. She's gonna conk out for sure when we get home tonight. She only slept for about a half hour before we came." His daughter now sat on her mother's lap, sucking her pointer finger.

"Poor baby," Leonora said as sleigh bells sounded from the front hall.

Lily's eyes grew big as saucers as she clung to Beth.

Beth kissed her rosy apple cheek. "Oh boy, Lil, guess who that is!"

"Santa!" Ben the third screamed as he hopped down and headed for the front hall.

Lang scooped Lily up and Harley Charlotte as they followed the squeals of delight toward the front door.

"Poor Mickey," Maggie whispered to Amy. "Thank goodness Spark has his plane standing by. He'll be glad to get out of town and rest with his family after all this."

Amy nodded. "He's such a, sweetheart. Doesn't mind a bit. He worships Dad and would do anything for him."

After Santa's departure, a wild hour of gift-giving ensued. Afterward, Maggie put a Christmas movie on for the children in the library, and the adults retreated to the living room and flopped down on sofas, chairs, and the thick-carpeted floor. Talk turned to England, and they began brainstorming ideas about the logistics of getting the entire crew across the country, then across the Atlantic.

Ned Williams sat on a love seat, hand casually draped around Wrenn's shoulders. Leonora peered over at the couple and smiled. "I hope you both are going to join us?"

Ned grinned. "I don't know, Nora. Someone's gotta stay back and hold down the fort."

"Nonsense! We've got that covered, don't we?" she said, turning first to her husband, then her eldest son.

Ben looked at his mother. "Gonna be dicey, if you want to know the truth. Jeb and Nick can take care of the stables."

"I thought Jeb and Amy would be coming too?" Leonora said.

"I wish," Jeb said, "but I'm in school. I can't afford to take the time off. Amy and Toby are going, though."

"Raoul's got a plan for the farm," Beth said. "Although I hate to burden him."

"He'll be fine," Ruthie said. "Mr. I Can't Leave Valley Stables for Long insists that we can only stay a week, so I'll be back to help too."

Leonora clapped her hands. "It's going to be such fun! I know we shouldn't allow you kids to pay for it, but we're so excited. And your mom's agreed to come too," she added, turning to Harriet. "I wish we could cajole Richard, Lucy, and the rest of your family into coming along too!"

"Pretty soon we'll have to reserve the entire hotel," Sam said. As he spoke, he gazed over at his wife and blanched. "Honey, what's wrong?"

"I think my water just broke," she said. "Oh Sam, this is too soon."

CHAPTER 27

"The ambulance is on its way, honey." Leonora said, hand on Sam's shoulder as he gently lay Rose on their bed. "How is she?"

"In pain, but she's strong. How long did they say?"

"It's coming from the other side of Grenville."

"Geez, Mom, that's at least an hour," he said, his dark brown eyes staring up at his mother.

Rose grimaced in pain, grasping his hand. "I won't make it, sweetie. Go down and get Wrenn, or even Kyle or Ned."

"Vets? You're asking for an acupuncturist or a vet?"

Normally calm and quiet, Rose sat up sharply, hazel eyes ablaze as she grabbed her husband's forearms. "Go and get them now!"

"Okay, okay, sweetie. I'll be right back."

Within minutes, Wrenn Parsons appeared, her red dress covered with a long, pristine white chef's apron. She sat on the edge of the bed, taking Rose's hand. "How're you doing?" she asked softly.

"Two minutes apart, and I feel like I need to push."

"Okay, okay... Let's start panting. Mrs. Morgan?" she asked, turning to face her hostess.

"Leonora, please, honey."

"We need lots of clean towels, hot water, clean scissors, and some facecloths. And please have someone call Chester Black. He's the nearest doctor. Also, see if anyone has a stethoscope handy."

"I have one. It's in my bag," Rose said, pointing across the room at an open suitcase. "Sam?"

As Sam retrieved the small medical bag Rose traveled with, Leonora hurried downstairs ignoring her creaking hips as she barked orders. Ben Senior called Chester, and Robbie offered to go into town and pick him up.

"No worries, son. He's on his way," his father said, pacing the floor.

A few minutes later, her contraction subsiding, Rose gazed around the room till she found Leonora. "Would you phone my mom? I was already so sad she couldn't be here today, but I know she'd want to be here now."

"Of course, honey. I'll go now," Leonora said, squeezing Sam's shoulder as she scurried from the room.

Leonora had barely disappeared when another strong contraction hit and Rose screamed. "I can't, I can't! It hurts too much."

Without a word, Sam slipped on the bed behind her and cradled her in his arms. "You can do it, baby. Just a little longer."

"Rose, I'm going to check and see what's happening, okay?" Wrenn said, moving to peek under the thin blanket covering Rose's knees. She poked her head out of sight, then instantly reappeared. She took a few seconds to place the stethoscope on Rose's belly, then said, "The head is right there. On the next contraction, you need to push."

Drenched in sweat, Rose shook her head back and forth. "No, no, no! We're waiting for the doctor!"

Wrenn took her hand. "We can't. The baby's heart rate has gotten weaker. He or she's ready to come."

"It's a girl," Sam said, kissing his wife's cheek and stroking her brow. "You can do this, sweetie."

Wrenn smiled at her, then took her place at the foot of the bed. "Big breath now and push with all you've got."

As the contraction began, Rose took a breath and pushed. Her face bright red from the strain, she dug her fingers into Sam's forearms as he held her tight.

"Great job," Wrenn said. "The head is out. One more big push and she'll be here!"

As the next contraction came over her, Rose pushed.

At that moment, her mother and Leonora appeared at the bedroom door. "Oh, my poor baby!" Martha cried, rushing to the opposite side of the bed, applying gobs of hand sanitizer, then grasping Rose's hand.

A baby's cry rang through the house as Wrenn wrapped a fluffy white towel around her. "What a beautiful girl!" she said, holding her up so the parents could see.

Tears streamed down Rose's face as Sam hugged and kissed her. "She's perfect, sweetie. Just like you."

"Would you like to cut the cord?" Wrenn asked him.

"Thanks, but my legs are too shaky. Not sure I could even stand. You better do it."

Wrenn tied, then cut the umbilical cord, wrapped the baby tight, and laid her on Rose's stomach just as Chester Black stepped into the room.

"Dr. Black, thank goodness," she said, standing up and ceding space to him.

"Looks like you're doin' just fine without me," he said.

"Afterbirth still to come," Wrenn said.

Black pulled on surgical gloves and knelt in Wrenn's place. "Good work, Ms. Parsons," he said. "You've done this before, haven't you?"

"Only with my sister. I assisted her midwife."

"Nothing more special than a Christmas baby," he said, smiling at the parents, who held the tiny infant. "Know what you're gonna call her?"

Rose gazed at her mother, then Leonora, before looking up at Sam. "With my husband's permission, I'd like to call her Wrenn Martha Nora Morgan. I know it's long, but what do you think?"

Sam kissed her nose. "It's perfect just like you and our sweet little Wrenn."

The acupuncturist stood nearby, eyes wide with disbelief, tears streaming down her cheeks.

"Oh," Rose said, "I'm sorry. I hope that's okay with you, Wrenn?"

Wrenn wiped her eyes with her apron. "It's more than okay. I'm honored beyond words."

"Good," Sam said. "Is there anyone else here who'd like to hold our Christmas baby?"

Martha came closer, and he handed the baby to her. "Oh, Nora, isn't she precious?" Martha said, tears in her eyes.

Leonora hugged her friend. "She sure is, darlin'."

After Leonora had held her for a short time, she said, "We've got a huge crowd waiting to meet this baby, and the ambulance just arrived. Could Martha or I carry her down so everyone could say hello before you take off?"

"Do we have to go to the hospital?" Rose said, gazing up at Chester Black. "I'd be so much more comfortable here."

"Don't see why you can't stay here. Placenta's intact, your vitals are good, and baby's in fine shape. I need to weigh her, but she looks to be about seven or eight pounds. Someone said she was early, but she sure doesn't look like it to me."

"Truth is we weren't sure," Rose said. "Pretty lame considering I'm a doctor. I'm afraid I've been so busy, I've missed my last two sonograms."

Black smiled. "No worries. Not an exact science even in this high-tech world. I'll send visiting nurses over in the morning, if you promise to stay put. No jumping around. Let someone help you to the bathroom and all."

"I promise," Rose said softly.

"Are you sure it's safe?" Sam asked.

"Probably safer than the hospital. Definitely more restful. But you've got to keep her down."

"No worries there," Sam said.

Leonora handed the baby to her son. "I think you should take her down to meet the family. We'll make sure they keep their distance. Chester, should I send the ambulance on its way, then?"

"Yes, tell 'em I okayed it. I'd like to stay with Rose a little longer. Then I'll weigh Wrenn and get out of your hair."

The collective ahhs and oohs when the baby appeared prompted a spontaneous round of Christmas carols, starting with "We Wish You a Merry Christmas."

Later, Wrenn weighed—seven pounds, nine ounces—and back in her parents' arms, the rest of the group prepared to head home. As people donned coats, jackets, and scarfs, Spark's voice rang out above the rest. "To the finest family in the world, God bless us everyone!"

"Got that right, buddy," Ben Senior said, clapping him on the shoulder. "We're blessed indeed."

CHAPTER 28

"House's pretty quiet," Spark said as he and Ben Senior sat in his sunporch drinking coffee.

"Ours too," his friend said. "You still in for dinner?"

"I'll be there."

"I've got the Lodge's quietest table reserved."

"Still just the three of us?" Spark asked as the phone rang. "You got it, Aria?" he called.

Ben nodded. "The kids like to stay home. I asked Martha and Jaybo, but they declined."

"Wish I could've gotten Helen back out. Next year," Spark said, gazing up as his chef came in.

"It's for you," she said. "Jonas Miller."

Spark looked up to find Aria's lovely features stricken with sadness. "What's he want, I wonder?"

She practically threw the phone at him and marched out of the room.

Spark covered the receiver and winked at his friend. "Trouble in paradise." Removing his hand, he said, "Hey, buddy, Happy New Year!"

Ben listened to the brief one-sided conversation. When Spark clicked off, he said, "Good news?"

His friend grinned. "Maybe, but I don't want to say anything and get her hopes up."

That evening, as he prepared to head over to Morgan's Run, Spark found his chef in the kitchen, a bowl of soup in front of her. "Sure you don't want to come with us, darlin'? Us old fogies would love a beautiful young lady at our table."

"Thanks, Spark, but I'm not crazy about New Year's Eve. I'm going to curl up and watch silly television shows with a gallon or two of ice cream."

He smiled at the woman who had become like another daughter to him. "Good plan. You sure you're okay?"

"What did he want?" she asked, both of them needing no clarification about who "he" was.

"Just checkin' in. Had a few questions about our new operation in Tucson, that's all."

"Really?"

"That's what he said."

"Does he want a job?"

Spark shrugged. He'd been in business long enough to know that Jonas Miller would be working for Foster Enterprises before the Tucson facility was fully operational, but he didn't want to create false hope. "Guess we'll have to see, won't we? Have a good evening, darlin'. I'll be back by nine at the latest. Us geezers don't do midnight anymore."

Aria gave him a wan smile. "Neither do us youngins. Have fun."

CHAPTER 29

"Happy New Year, dear Spark," Leonora said as the friends walked arm in arm through the Lodge. The annual New Year's Eve party was in full swing with guests who made the annual pilgrimage to the inn. Every room was taken, several by celebrities who had been spending the holiday in Saguaro for many years. As the friends strolled through the dining room and across the lobby, people greeted them, begging them to stay and party.

Spark chuckled. "I feel like a party pooper leavin' so early, but truth is after that meal and two weeks of partying, this ole guy is pooped."

"Me too!" Ben said. "But I sure hate to admit it."

Leonora nodded at a passerby, then whispered, "Pooh, you two. We've been coming to this for forty years. We can slip out whenever we please."

"Evenin', folks," Jim Thompson, the Lodge manager, said. "Off so soon?" The debonair dark-haired man gave a slight bow. In his midfifties, Jim had been at the ranch almost eighteen years. He prided himself on his appearance and was always impeccably dressed whether in upscale ranch duds or business casual. Tonight he looked especially dapper in a tuxedo, red bow tie, and cummerbund.

"'Fraid so, Jim," Ben said, shaking his hand. "You, Bebe, and the crew have outdone yourselves again. Everything was perfect."

Jim smiled. "Thanks, boss."

Leonora hugged and kissed both the manager's cheeks. "Please tell George how much we enjoyed the meal. I normally don't like to eat those sweet little quail, but I make an exception on New Year's Eve."

George Baran, their chef, had earned the Lodge five-star ratings many times over the years. Tonight's six-course meal began with creamy leek soup, then a light fish course of trout crusted with pistachios. Then the first of two sorbet palate-cleansing breaks before the main course, the wine-braised quail. A vegetable gratin followed, then a second sorbet, before an endive salad, pots de crème, and a platter of local cheeses and fruits. Each course was served on the Lodge's signature china, handcrafted by a local potter. Even the delicate sorbet plates with the tiny depression in the center for the ball of sorbet depicted the desert flora and fauna against an off-white background, the iconic saguaro cactuses in full bloom.

Jim bowed again. "I will be sure to tell him. Enjoy the rest of your evening, folks."

∾

"I was surprised that none of the kids came tonight," Leonora said as her husband helped her out of her moss-green wool coat and hung it in the front hall closet.

"Not their scene, what with little kids and all," he said, drawing her close and kissing her.

"Yes, but they sometimes make an appearance."

"You looked beautiful tonight," he said. And she did in a shimmery pale green top, white wool pencil skirt, and three-inch heels.

"Thanks, handsome. You did too."

"Nightcap?"

"Only if we can have it upstairs in bed."

"Champagne or…?"

"A tiny glass of amaretto?"

"Comin' up. You go on, I'll get the drinks and be right up."

As Ben rummaged in the liquor cupboard, he thought back to the day he and Nora moved to Saguaro. Just graduated and almost free of debt, the young rancher proudly carried her over the threshold of the cabin he had had restored as a surprise for his bride.

"Close your eyes, darlin'," he'd said as they drove up the winding drive to the ramshackle dwelling he had worked on for four years. The future home of Raoul and Carmela, the newlyweds were destined to spend a year there while their own home was built. Later, more cabins were added to Morgan's Run, including their secret cabin, a gift from Ben on their tenth anniversary. Long ago the cabin and the old farmhouse were the only buildings on the ranch.

He helped her from the car, kissing her temple. "Keep those eyes shut!"

"Where are we?"

"You'll see!" He led her up the path to the cabin door.

After carrying her over the threshold, he whispered, "Welcome home, sweetheart."

Leonora opened her eyes to find a warm, inviting space. The rustic wood-paneled living room, dining room, and kitchen was furnished simply, a cheery fire burning in the blue enamel wood stove. Two bedrooms and a bath were off the back hallway. He carried her into the first and set her gently on the wrought iron bed that was covered in a quilt of soft greens and blue. Aside from the bed, the room's furnishings consisted of two wooden dressers and small matching tables on either side of the bed. In lieu of closets, three of the walls were lined with wooden peg racks, hangers for their clothes dangling from each peg.

"It won't be for long. I promise," he said, leaning over to kiss her.

"It's perfect," she said softly, arms circling his neck, drawing him closer. "And I'd happily spend the rest of my life here if we're together."

"I doubt that, Nora from Bel Air, but I love you for saying so." He eased down beside her, stroking her hair.

"I'm not Nora from Bel Air and never was, but I love you very much," she whispered, kissing him deeply. "And now it's time to christen this spanking-new bed. What do you say, cowboy?"

"Ben!" she called, disturbing his reverie. "Whatever are you doing?"

He grinned, grabbing the amaretto bottle and two small crystal glasses. "Comin', darlin'!"

When he stepped into the bedroom, she was at the window, gazing out at the stars. At the sound of his footsteps, she turned. She wore a pale pink floor-length gossamer gown, its plunging neckline and diaphanous material leaving little to the imagination. The soft, round curves of her body were framed in the lamplight as she stepped away from the window.

Ben whistled. "Wow! I haven't seen that one before!"

"No, you haven't, because I had Gabriela order it specially for tonight. I figured after the butcher chops my leg up next week, making love might be tricky for a while."

"Where there's a will, there's a way," he said, voice husky. "And I officially love Gabriella."

"Over here, cowboy," she said, crooking her finger.

Ben set the glasses and bottle down and crossed the room in two strides, swooping her up in his strong arms, setting her down on the bed. "Gladly, Mrs. Morgan. Whaddya say? Should we have a drink, or christen that new frock?"

"What do you think?" she said, kissing him, smiling as she felt him already hard against her. "Someone's raring to go."

"Don't you know it," he said, hands all over her, one easing the neckline of her nightie aside to cup her soft full breast. His lips moved down her neck to take her into his mouth, tongue teasing her nipple to exquisite hardness.

Leonora sighed, giving herself to him, her body suffused with warmth and desire. As he set her on the bed, she kissed his neck then found his lips. Ben slipped the gown over her head in one smooth move. Then he looked down at himself. "Guess I'd better get rid of these duds, doncha think?"

"If you don't, I'm gonna rip 'em off you." As he undressed, she laughed, caressing his leg, her hand moving upward as he slipped his boxers down.

"What're you chuckling about?"

"Frock? Ben Morgan, haven't I taught you anything about fashion in the past forty years?"

"Only that the best fashions slip on and off real easy." He parted her legs, moving between them to enter her in the exquisite dance they knew so well. "Happy New Year sweetie pie," he whispered.

"Happy New Year, my love."

"In case I forget to tell you after—thank you, darlin'."

Leonora gazed into his blue eyes and saw tears that matched her own. "You're welcome, cowboy."

Updates about future releases, please visit my AUTHOR WEBSITE and sign up for my Newsletter and Follow me on BookBub!

Please read on for sample chapters of *Aria's Song!*

ARIA'S SONG

Chapter 1

"Thanks for watching Toby," Amy Barnes said as she slipped onto a stool in her father's gleaming, state-of-the-art kitchen. They could see her nine-year-old, Toby, in his wheelchair, hunched over a table in his grandfather's sunroom, building a huge Lego structure. Ordinarily, Amy would not have asked her father's chef to babysit, but Aria had offered.

"No problem," Aria said. "He's a doll. Hardly knew he was here. How'd your doctor's appointment go?"

Amy blushed. "Fine, great. Where's Dad anyway?"

Aria noticed her companion's face redden, but decided it wasn't her place to ask. She knew her employer's daughter well, but they'd never really been friends. "Off with the other silver fox. They're out at the farm, I think." Aria referred to the thoroughbred farm Spark Foster and Ben Morgan had launched a year earlier just north of town.

Amy smiled. "They're something, aren't they?"

"They're amazing. If your dad's not out there, he's in Tucson overseeing the new headquarters. I don't know where he gets the energy."

Amy threw up her hands, laughing. "From the sun, of course!" Her billionaire father owned one of the world's most successful engineering firms, specializing in solar, wind, and hydroelectric power.

Aria raised her iced tea in toast. "Good one."

"So how are you doing anyway? Dad tells me you've joined the Valley Chorus."

"Had to do something to pretend to have a life."

Amy's kind eyes regarded her. "You'll get there. I know you miss Harriet." Harriet Morgan had come to Saguaro Valley with her mother, Helen, and the two women had become close in a very short time.

"Big-time. I miss my Portland gang too. I may head up for a visit in a few weeks, but in the meantime, I'm trying to make connections here. I've gone on a few of the Rambler Sports hikes."

"I've heard they're a fun group. Does Lang lead them?" Lang Dillon, a local boy, had come home to the Valley to marry Beth Morgan. She was the oldest daughter of Ben Morgan, one of the silver foxes. Lang owned Rambler Sports West, a mostly mail-order sporting goods store with an office in town.

"Rarely. His assistant, Barb, leads most of them. She's terrific. Spark says that Robbie Morgan's about to partner up with Lang to start offering full-fledged adventure tours, so that's something to look forward to." Robbie, Lang's brother-in-law, had also moved home to Saguaro after working for an adventure tour company in Sedona.

"I'll say. I'd love to take one of their tours. Well, there you go. You're getting out there!"

Aria smiled. *Could I be anymore pathetic?* "And—wait for this—I joined the Scrabble Club at the community center!"

"Really? I love Scrabble."

"You should come some night. We meet Sundays at six thirty and sometimes during the week, usually Wednesdays. It's me and mostly Valley seniors, but I love it and them."

"I will. So, if it's not too personal, what about that handsome Jonas Miller? Dad tells me he's here full-time now."

Aria blanched. "Sore subject. We had a very brief fling last year, that's all. Haven't seen or heard from him since he moved to Tucson."

"I'm surprised Dad hasn't had him out to the house."

"He has, and I make it a point to be out. Too awkward." *And the sight of him would rip my heart out.* "So enough about me. How are you and Jeb doing? Haven't seen much of you or him." Amy was a physical therapist who worked in Tucson, and Jeb was a stable hand at Morgan's Run, Ben Morgan's ranch. He had also recently started working on an engineering degree.

"He's super busy juggling work and school, and I'm really busy at the clinic. We're short-staffed right now. Thank goodness for the Cottage, you, Dad, and this community, or we could never do it. And now..." Amy touched her belly, gazing over at her. "Oh... Aria, I have to tell someone. It was such a shock and—"

"You're not?"

"I am! Just found out this morning. Jeb doesn't know. Toby either," she whispered. "I feel like such a traitor telling you before them, but I've never been good at keeping secrets, and this has come out of nowhere."

"So you weren't trying?"

Amy leaned closer. "Well, yes, we were. We've been trying for two years. That's the thing. We've been to doctors and tried everything. We'd kind of given up."

"Isn't that when people often get pregnant? When they give up trying?"

Amy shrugged. "I guess, but if we think our life's busy now, what will a baby mean?"

"Hey, Mom!" Toby called as he twirled his wheelchair around and headed in their direction.

Amy stood. "Mum's the word." Her companion nodded as Amy turned to her son. "Hey, baby, you ready to go grab some lunch? Maybe Aria would like to join us? I thought we'd eat at Gracie's."

"Thanks, guys, but I've got a ton of work here this morning."

"Don't let Grandpa touch that," Toby said, pointing toward the sunroom. "I want to finish it myself."

Aria smiled, ruffling his hair. "No worries, I'll watch him like a hawk."

As mother and child headed out, she sighed, bringing the empty glasses to the sink. *Will I ever have that? What joy Amy and Jeb have together, with their adopted son Toby and now a baby on the way?*

The house Spark's people had found Jonas was in a great location, just off Reid Park, in the Sam Hughes area southeast of downtown Tucson. There were great restaurants within walking distance, and the Foster Enterprises complex was a fifteen-minute drive into the Catalina Foothills. Gregarious by nature, Jonas was already on a first-name basis with the staff at the nearby natural foods market and corner deli. After years of constant travel, it felt good to stay put for a while, but if he was being honest, he wasn't much of a city boy, and he missed wide open spaces. Saguaro Valley and a certain violet-eyed chef were what had tempted him to come West. Of course, the huge salary Spark offered him didn't hurt either. He enjoyed his trips north and was looking forward to the evening ahead. He hoped that finally, on this visit, Aria would be home.

Growing up in Horseshoe Crab Cove, Jonas and a couple of his brothers were considered the local heartthrobs. He'd certainly had his share of girlfriends over the last two decades and had even lived with a couple of them, including Alli, his graduate school girlfriend. Alli was now married to Nick, another longtime friend, and they had just welcomed their fourth child. *What's wrong with you, buddy? Have you lost out on life? Missed the boat?*

It had been a weird few years for the forty-two-year-old engineer. In his previous job, he'd spent a good deal of time in Austin, Texas, long enough to form a relationship with a coworker, a relationship he'd never shared with family or friends. A manager at the Austin office, Selena Montgomery was known as the Ice Queen, hard and unapproachable. Jonas had viewed her reputation as a challenge, and it hadn't taken long before *she* was pursuing *him*. As their relationship grew, he abandoned his usual hotel. Whenever he was in town, he would stay at Selena's modern chrome-and-leather-furnished condo, a stark, gleaming, minimalist space that mirrored the woman herself.

He shuddered recalling their inevitable breakup, his belongings strewn on the sidewalk as the redheaded harridan screamed and cursed, flinging items from the windows ten stories up. It had been over a year since that day, and he was still gun-shy, leery of getting close to another woman just yet. This was partially responsible for his hands-off, fly-the-coop behavior after sharing a passionate few days with Aria Firorelli. *What a shit I was*, he thought. *Why wouldn't she make herself scarce every time I come to the Valley? Maybe someday soon I'll catch her, and then we'll see.*

His cell rang. When he answered, Drew Martin, his new colleague, said, "Hey, buddy, pick you up at five?"

"Great, thanks, Drew." He clicked off and threw the phone on the bed. *Time to take a run before the heat does me in.*

Chapter 2

"Hey, gal, how're ya doin'?" Spark called as he stepped into the kitchen, finding his chef chopping vegetables. "Something smells good."

"I'm making you a beef ragout tonight," she said. "Just got the ranch order this morning." She referred to their weekly share of produce and meat from Morgan's Run.

"Sounds great, darlin'. Did I tell you I've got a couple of the Tucson crew comin'? Your friend Jonas Miller and a couple of his new coworkers. We'd love for you to join us."

She blanched, turning away so he wouldn't see her dismay. "Thanks, but it's my chorus practice. If it's okay, I'll get everything prepared and head off about five?"

"More than okay. It's your night off, so you do what you like. Don't even have to prepare dinner. We can always head over to the Lodge."

"Whatever you prefer," she said, turning to smile at him. After so much time together, her boss was more like a benevolent uncle, and she loved him more than her own parents.

He patted her hand. "Your stew will do just fine. You can't hide from him forever, you know."

"What are you talking about?"

"I know it's none of my business, but I could tell you and the charming Mr. Miller had a little something going when he was here for the holidays last year."

You're right. It is none of your business, she thought as she slapped carrots on the cutting board and began chopping furiously. "A very short something. He couldn't get out of town fast enough."

"Don't know about that, but I do know he's always askin' about you."

"Spark, I know you mean well, but I'm trying to bring balance to my life, not heartache."

Her employer frowned. "Did he take liberties with you? If yes, I'll fire him on the spot."

She grinned. "All's well. My virtue is intact, never fear. Now what can I get you for lunch? I have pastrami, tuna salad, and turkey. I could also make grilled cheese or bacon?"

"You know, I think I'll have a grilled cheese and a cup of your excellent tomato soup, if there's any left."

Aria set down her knife. "Coming right up. Where'll you be?"

He pointed to the sunroom. "I'm just gonna grab my book. No hurry."

"Five minutes. And your grandson said don't touch anything on the Lego table."

Spark chuckled. "Spoil sport. I was just thinkin' of putting my engineering skills to work and finishing it up."

"Better not. He was very adamant."

Jonas, Drew, and their other two coworkers, Ginger Wingate and Fiona Rawls, arrived at their boss's sprawling estate a little after five that evening, the sun blazing, a light breeze blowing across the surprisingly green fields that stretched behind the house all the way to the mountains.

"Wow," Ginger exclaimed. It was her first visit to the Valley. "I mean, wow! This is incredible. How do they keep it so green?"

Jonas grinned, leaning on the hood of Drew's jeep as he gazed west at the beautiful scenery before them. "It's called an orographic effect. The valley has an unusual cloud cover that traps moisture, or the mountains on either side trap moisture, I guess. All I know is this area stays green all year. You should see the Morgan's Run organic farm. Hundreds of green acreage just like this."

She sighed. "Heaven." Ginger was from Seattle, and she missed the rain and the green.

"Welcome!" their host called from the front steps. "Come on up."

As Spark gave them the five-cent tour, as he called it, Jonas peered into the kitchen for signs of Aria, but the house appeared to be empty except for his boss. When Spark noticed his gaze, he said, "She's not here, buddy."

For a split second, Jonas considered playing dumb, pretending not to understand Spark's meaning, but then just shrugged. "Hope she's not avoiding me."

The others had gone on ahead and were oohing and ahhing at the enormous living room and dining room. Spark paused, then said, "There may be some of that."

"I don't blame her. I was a world-class jerk."

His boss chuckled. "I doubt that. Maybe just confused?"

Jonas grinned. "Yeah, right. Is that how they describe idiotic assholes out here in the valley?"

"No, but we do believe in second chances."

"How can I get a chance if I never see her?"

"I've always found that chances worth their salt are seldom by chance," Spark said, patting his shoulder. "There's always the phone. Come on, let's corral the others for a drink before we tour the barns. What do you say?"

Chapter 3

It was after nine when Aria headed home from chorus practice. Spark had indicated that his guests had to be on the road early, so Aria decided she was safe. As she drove the short distance home, she thought back to the memorable evening when she'd lost her virginity to Jonas Miller. Thirty-one and still a virgin, that had been her, the flirting and flamboyant behavior an act to hide the scared young girl she still was. After watching her mother fling herself at one man after another through four marriages and her sister Marana's string of loser boyfriends, Aria had avoided having sex through her teens and twenties. She always broke up with boyfriends as soon as the inevitable "doing it" crept into their conversation.

She'd escaped more times than she could count, until she met Jonas Miller. The tall, dark-haired Easterner with his slate-gray eyes had blown her away the first time she laid eyes on him. If she had to lose her virginity, this was the man to help her, she decided. Then a slow, sensual dance at Kyle and Harriet Morgan's wedding reception had led to their lovemaking. Thoughts of it were still enough to send her into orbit.

Lost in thought, she'd driven in and parked without checking the front driveway for cars. As she opened the kitchen door, she heard voices and assumed Spark was watching television. As she began to clear dishes from the counter, the door to the dining room swung open, and there he was—platters and dishes in each hand. "Hey! Aria, finally!" he said, his eyes sparkling with warmth.

"Hello," she mumbled, eyes lowered.

He came forward, setting down his load and circling the island. "I've been hoping to see you."

Before she knew it, his arms were around her. For an instant, she gave herself to him, basking in his warmth and comforted by the strength of his embrace. *Home,* she thought, breathing in his scent of musk and spices. Then, coming to her senses, she stepped back.

"Yes... Well, I've been busy. I've joined a local chorus, and they have lots of practices, and I'm in a hiking group and a bunch of other activities." She knew she was rambling and that her face must be beet red, but she couldn't stop herself.

He watched her, his gaze kind and soft. "Hey, I'm sorry I haven't been in touch."

She shrugged. "I'm sure the new job has kept you busy."

"It has, but I'd really like to see you. I want to—"

The door swung open, and two strangers stepped in, one a medium-built, round-faced guy with sandy hair and wire-rimmed glasses, his companion, tall and curvaceous, with glorious long auburn hair.

"Hey, buddy, time we were hitting it," Drew said, his gaze firmly on Aria, not his coworker. "Is this the famous chef we heard so much about over dinner?"

Jonas turned to his colleagues. "Ginger, Drew, this is Aria Firorelli. Aria, these are my colleagues."

As the others exchanged greetings and shook hands, he asked, "Where's Fiona?"

Ginger waved a hand dismissively, flipping a lock of her curly auburn hair. "Ms. Nosey asked Spark for a tour of the second floor. I got bored after the fourth bedroom and headed back to find you two. Aria, your dinner was fabulous. I'd love the recipe for that amazing beef bourguignon,"

Aria smiled. "It's just a simple ragout, but I'm happy to share how I make it. The secret is the beef, which is grass fed and locally grown. It's what makes it special."

"I'll say," Ginger went on, as if the men had disappeared. She was now perched on one of the barstools and had crossed her thin legs in black capris. Her red sandals with their six-inch heels clattered against the legs of her seat. "Tell me more."

Wondering what there was to add, Aria opened her mouth to speak, but was saved by her boss, who stepped into the room behind a short, dark-haired woman in leggings and tunic, sensible flats on her tiny feet. "Hey, honey, you're back. Your dinner got rave reviews. Did you meet this gal?"

"No, hello," Aria said, coming forward to greet the newcomer. "I'm

Aria, Spark's chef." She extended her hand, which the other woman took, giving her a dead-fish handshake.

"Fiona Rawls. Great dinner."

"Thanks. I didn't mean to interrupt you all. I'll clean up and be out of your way."

The interplay between his chef and newest employee was not lost on Spark, who clapped his hands and said, "How 'bout a nightcap, everyone? Darlin', you join us too. Leave that till tomorrow."

Aria smiled at him, her employer's motives crystal clear. The kindest, most generous person she knew, once you were part of Spark's world—employee or friend—you instantly became family. And Spark devoted practically every waking minute to making his family happy. She knew he regarded her as a daughter and probably felt the same about his four dinner guests.

"Thanks, Spark, but I feel a headache coming on. I'm going to soak these dishes and head off to bed."

With a wink, he said, "Of course, darlin'. We'll get out of your hair."

"We've gotta hit the road anyway," Drew said. Fiona and Ginger didn't look in any hurry to depart.

As the group said goodbye and shuffled out of the kitchen, Jonas stepped close to her and whispered, "I'll call. I'd really like to see you. Have dinner or something?"

"Nice to see you," she said. "Better catch up with your friends."

When the door closed behind them, Aria let out her breath in a whoosh. *The man is as hot as ever. How will I ever say no if he calls?*

Get *Aria's Song*!

ALSO BY M. LEE PRESCOTT

Contemporary Romance

Mystery

The Ricky Steele Mysteries

Prepped to Kill

Gadfly

Lost in Spindle City

Poof!

Lady Love: A Cautionary Tale

Also, featuring Ricky Steele:

Jigsaw

Roger and Bess Mysteries

A Friend of Silence

In the Name of Silence

The Silence of Memory

Silencing the Pen

Well-Loved Romances

Widow's Island

Hestor's Way

Morgan's Run Romances

Emma's Dream

Lang's Return

Jeb's Promise

Rose's Choice

Hope's Wonder

Ruthie's Love

Polly's Heart

Kyle's Journey

Gus' Home

A Valley Christmas

Aria's Song

Tom's Ride

Bella's Touch

Morgan's Fire Romances

Lucy's Hearth

Tim's Hands

Pam's Garden

Rich's Dilemma

Lolly's Wish

Greta's Goat

A Horseshoe Crab Cove Christmas

Joe's Calling

Young Adult Historical Romance

Song of the Spirit

A NOTE FROM THE AUTHOR

I am so happy to bring you *A Valley Christmas*. The tenth **Morgan's Run** title, *A Valley Christmas* is Ben and Leonora's love story. At its conclusion is a sneak preview of number eleven—*Aria's Song*. Be sure to check out my spin-off series, Morgan's Fire, another contemporary romance series that follows Helen, Harriet, and a host of strong, resilient women across the country to the New England coastal town of Horseshoe Crab Cove.

Thank you so much for reading *A Valley Christmas* and celebrating the holidays, Kyle and Harriet's wedding and Ben and Leonora's fortieth wedding anniversary with me in Saguaro Valley. As you know, the **Morgan's Run** books are set in the gorgeous American Southwest, an area of the country that is dear to my heart not only because it is home to my youngest son and family, but also because its beauty is so extraordinary and so startlingly different from that of my New England home. Now I am loving exploring the beauty of the craggy New England coast with a village of colorful, vibrant characters of **Morgan's Fire!**

If you like *A Valley Christmas* and would be willing to write an Amazon review, I would be very grateful. If you would like to sign up for future book releases, giveaways, and occasional notices about my books, please visit my Author Website *http://www.mleeprescott.com/*

and sign up for my newsletter and follow me on BookBub *https://www.bookbub.com/search/authors?search=M.+Lee+Prescott.* I promise I will not share your address, nor will I flood you with emails. Do visit my site to read more about my books and hear what's next.

Finally, this book has been revised, proofed, and edited many, many times, but my intrepid assistants and I are human, so if you spot a typo, please email me at *mleeprescott@gmail.com,* and I will fix it. If you'd like to know more about my other books, please scroll ahead to the next section.

Warm wishes and happy holidays!

M. Lee

ABOUT THE AUTHOR

M. Lee Prescott is the author of dozens of works of fiction for adults, young adults, and children, among them *Prepped to Kill*, *Gadfly*, *Lost in Spindle City*, and *Poof!* (Ricky Steele Mysteries), *A Friend of Silence*, *In the Name of Silence*, and *The Silence of Memory* (Roger and Bess Mysteries), *Jigsaw*, and *Song of the Spirit*, and her contemporary romance series, Morgan's Run, of which *A Valley Christmas* is the tenth! She is thrilled to also have three titles in her new spin-off romance series Morgan's Fire all published in 2019! Three of her nonfiction titles have been published by Heinemann, and she has published numerous articles in the field of literacy education. Lee is a professor of education at a small New England liberal arts college, where she teaches reading and writing pedagogy. Her current research focuses on mindfulness and connections to reading and writing. She regularly teaches abroad, most recently in Singapore.

Lee has lived in southern California (loved those Laguna nights!), Chapel Hill, North Carolina, and various spots in Massachusetts and Rhode Island. Currently, she resides in Massachusetts on a beautiful river, where she canoes, swims, and watches an incredible variety of wildlife pass by. She is the mother of two grown sons and spends lots of time with them, their beautiful wives, and her beloved grandchildren. When not teaching or writing, Lee's passions revolve around family, yoga (Kripalu is a second home), swimming, sharing mindfulness with children and adults, and walking.

Lee loves to hear from readers. Email her at *mleeprescott@gmail.com*, and visit her website to hear the latest and sign up for her newsletters!

Visit my author website and sign up for my newsletter at
http://www.mleeprescott.com.

Follow me on BookBub *https://www.bookbub.com/search/authors?
search=M.+Lee+Prescott*!

If you have five minutes, please review this book!

www.ingramcontent.com/pod-product-compliance
Lightning Source LLC
Chambersburg PA
CBHW061218210726
48294CB00006B/1890